DIE AFTER DARK

ALSO BY HUGH PENTECOST

Julian Quist Mystery Novels:

HONEYMOON WITH DEATH
THE JUDAS FREAK
THE BEAUTIFUL DEAD
THE CHAMPAGNE KILER
DON'T DROP DEAD TOMORROW

Pierre Chambrun Mystery Novels:

TIME OF TERROR
BARGAIN WITH DEATH
WALKING DEAD MAN
BIRTHDAY, DEATHDAY
THE DEADLY JOKE
GIRL WATCHER'S FUNERAL
THE GILDED NIGHTMARE
THE GOLDEN TRAP
THE EVIL MEN DO
THE SHAPE OF FEAR
THE CANNIBAL WHO OVERATE

John Jericho Mystery Novels:

A PLAGUE OF VIOLENCE
THE GIRL WITH SIX FINGERS
DEAD WOMAN OF THE YEAR
THE CREEPING HOURS
HIDE HER FROM EVERY EYE
SNIPER

Hugh Pentecost

DIE AFTER DARK

A Red Badge Novel of Suspense

DODD, MEAD & COMPANY, NEW YORK

Copyright © 1976 by Judson Philips
All rights reserved
No part of this book may be reproduced in any form
without permission in writing from the publisher
Printed in the United States of America
by The Haddon Craftsmen, Inc., Scranton, Penna.

Library of Congress Cataloging in Publication Data

Philips, Judson Pentecost,date
Die after dark.

(A Red badge novel of suspense)
I. Title.
PZ3.P5412Di [PS3531.H442] 813'.5'2 76-25558
ISBN 0-396-07345-X

PART ONE

CHAPTER ONE

Looking at him, you would write Julian Quist down as a complete extrovert. His very mod clothes, his golden hair worn long but carefully styled, his tendency toward bright-colored shirts, gave him the look of a man who dressed to be seen. This was a flamboyant man, you might have guessed, a skillful and professional show-off. But if you looked at him less casually you would have noticed that his pale blue eyes could take on a hard cold light, showed that he was assessing, shrewdly, what he heard and saw. If you had something to tell him you would find, unexpectedly perhaps, that he was a very good listener.

Andrew Crown needed someone to listen. He was in big trouble.

"Before I have finished telling you what's on my mind, Julian," Crown said, "you may decide to throw me to the wolves. But I'd appreciate it if you'd hear me out."

"That's what you pay me for," Quist said. "And in our ball game, Andrew, I need to know you better than I know my own brother—if I had one."

"It's a woman," Crown said.

"Old and ugly, I trust," Quist said.

"Middle-aged—prime of life. Very lush, very lovely, very special, I thought."

Quist leaned back in his desk chair, his eyes narrowed. "It's a little late for you to turn up with indiscretions," he said.

"God help me," Crown said.

The offices of Julian Quist Associates are located high above Grand Central Station in New York City in a great glass finger that points to the sky. It is as modern in its furnishings and its personnel as Quist's wardrobe. The business is public relations. Quist calls himself an image maker. He creates images for theater people, movie stars, athletes, writers, diplomats, businesses, new products on the market. One thing Julian Quist Associates had usually steered away from was politics. But this was a political year and Andrew Crown was in the political arena. Andrew Crown, in his fifties, was about to launch a campaign he hoped would take him to the United States Senate. Julian Quist might just be the man who could get him there.

Several years ago when Quist, just thirty, was starting to write his name across the public relations sky, he had met Andrew Crown. Crown was the attorney for a group of men who were launching a big new sports arena on Long Island. Quist had been engaged to help sell the venture to the public. He had found Andrew Crown to be a very competent lawyer, also a man with a nice sense of humor and a pleasant supply of compassion in a throat-cutting, competitive world. When the job was over, Quist and Crown had maintained a friendship—a lunch together now and then, a visit to some event at the Sports Arena. They didn't go to each other's homes. Andrew Crown's wife, Marjorie, had been tragically crippled in an automobile accident and was permanently anchored to a wheelchair. She had shut herself off from the world. She wouldn't leave her bedroom and sitting room in the Crowns' house on Long Island. She wouldn't receive guests there. It

4

was a tragedy for her and a tragedy for Andrew. He was a very alive, vital, and gregarious man. Politics, Quist had agreed, might be an answer for him. It would keep him constantly on the go, in contact with busy, active people. Quist thought Andrew had a very good chance to beat out the conservative incumbent. But not with a scandal hanging over his head.

"You've gotten your lady pregnant and she's about to blackmail you. Is that it?" Quist asked.

Crown shook his head slowly. He was a stocky man with salt-and-pepper brown hair and a sad round face that could light up with a boyish smile when he was able to pull himself out of a kind of perpetual gloom.

"The lady and I have never had any sexual experience together. Not that I didn't dream of it. Not that I didn't want it! God, Julian, can you imagine what it's like to be cut off as a man when it is just autumn and there is still time for you to have and enjoy what may be the very best of it. Marjorie's accident—"

"Perhaps we'd better stop playing around with this and you tell me what it is," Quist said.

"It's disaster," Crown said.

He told his story.

One afternoon about a year ago he found himself with a free morning. He had driven to his club to play nine holes of golf. The course was usually quite empty on a weekday morning. He had been very short on exercise lately, so he set out alone, pulling his clubs in a little carrier. He had sliced a shot off the third tee and a woman had popped out of the woods. She'd been hunting for her ball and Crown's errant tee shot had missed her by inches. She was good-humored about it. She was on the short side, blonde, with a trim, rather lush figure. She introduced herself as Allegra Landis. Mrs. Allegra Landis. Early forties, Crown thought. Did he mind if she played along with him? He didn't mind at all.

There are men who enjoy women without being lechers, who enjoy the pleasure of mild flirtation without any serious design. Crown was such a man, and the byplay with women had been pretty well cut out of his life by Marjorie's accident. He didn't go to parties any more. He stayed at home with his unhappy wife. Because he loved her; because until that ghastly night when a runaway trailer truck hit her car broadside she had been a marvelous companion, everything he had ever needed or wanted sexually. She had been a perfect lover.

But now Crown needed, more than he knew, some kind of female companionship. He didn't imagine that it would amount to any more than playing the next six holes of golf with Allegra Landis. In the hour that it took to play those six holes and the hour they spent afterwards in the club grill having Bloody Marys, Crown found Allegra charming, outgoing, ready to laugh at his sly witticisms. He hated to have it come to an end. It had been a most pleasant interlude.

Toward the end it developed that she knew who he was. She was the legal secretary for another lawyer whom Crown knew quite well. She knew about Marjorie. Allegra had her own problems. She was forty-three years old. She admitted it quite frankly, perhaps because she didn't look forty-three. She had been married to one man for twenty-five years. A child bride, she called herself. She had two grown sons, scattered somewhere. A year ago her husband had asked for a divorce.

"He found himself a sexy chick," Allegra said.

"He already had a sexy chick, didn't he?" Crown asked. It was just a polite form of flirtation.

"It's hard to pick yourself up off the floor," Allegra said. "There's never been any other man in my life. Now that I'm divorced I find I'm a target for every stud in the neighborhood."

"You can't really blame them," Crown said, still just flirtatiously polite.

6

For the first time she seemed suddenly tense. "I'm just not ready for anything yet. I'm just not ready."

"The right guy will come along," Crown said.

She thanked him for having let her join him. He thanked her. It had been his pleasure. He was sorry to watch her drive off because he supposed that was that.

It never occurred to Crown that he would be unfaithful to Marjorie. But the little passage with Allegra Landis made him realize how much he missed the simple pleasure of female companionship without the gloom and despair that now surrounded Marjorie. He found himself thinking about her long after she should have been forgotten.

About a week after the golf morning he found himself looking for her name in the telephone book. It wasn't there. There was a James Landis. She might still be living in the house she had shared with her husband. He tried it. A crisp female answered, told him that Allegra Landis no longer lived there. Information might be able to give him her number. Information could and did.

She sounded pleased to hear from him. She had rented the guest cottage on a big estate, the horsey Bradens. Would he like to stop by for a drink?

He was suddenly a conspirator. He called Marjorie. Work was going to keep him late.

"Why in God's name should you come home to me, Andrew?" Marjorie asked with all her accumulated bitterness.

"I won't be late, darling."

"Oh, Andrew, Andrew, Andrew."

He should have gone home then. He didn't.

The guest cottage on the Braden estate was something out of a child's fairy story, Crown told Julian Quist.

"Hidden away in a clump of willow trees, flowers everywhere, wisteria vines," Crown said.

All he saw of it that first evening was sort of kitchen-living room that took up the whole ground floor of the cottage.

There was a stove and refrigerator and a china cabinet and a door that led into a pantry. But there were also filled bookcases, and a hi-fi record and tape player and a little bar on wheels.

Allegra seemed genuinely glad to see him. She was small, with delicate bones, probably not weighing much over a hundred pounds, Crown thought. But the pale green dress she wore was so exquisitely fitted to her figure that she looked more opulent than she actually was.

She made him a martini. He suggested they go out somewhere for dinner. She just happened to have a steak and salad makings in the icebox. Wouldn't he prefer to picnic here?

He had scanned the bookcase while she made the martinis. She read novels mostly, he saw. Not the most recent. She clearly wasn't a book club subscriber. He remembered later that she had remarked that things were pretty tight financially. She couldn't afford books these days. He thought the husband who had run off with the chick should be paying enough alimony to justify the buying of books. He didn't mention it then, but sometime later she said she wouldn't take money from Jim Landis. She preferred independence. When her husband walked out she'd been lucky enough to get a job with Eliot Keyes, the lawyer Crown knew. She had worked for Keyes some years before and he was glad to take her on as a sort of girl Friday. He had found her this cottage on the Braden estate. The Bradens were friends of Keyes'.

It was a night for personal histories. He told her about Marjorie, transformed overnight from a wonderful gay and vital woman into an embittered and nearly helpless cripple. Her life destroyed; his life emptied of everything but his work and care of and pity for the woman he loved. Not really the woman he loved, but a grim caricature of the once vibrant Marjorie.

Allegra talked about her marriage to Jim Landis. She had been eighteen when she married a glamorous man-about-town in a small town, ten years her senior. It had been, she thought, a perfect marriage. She had borne him two sons, had two miscarriages, thought their love life, apparently very active, was perfect. Then, out of the blue, a twenty-year-old chick and smashup.

She and Crown were alike, Allegra thought. Each trying to make a new life on the wreckage of something they'd thought was perfect.

That was the beginning. Crown began to "work late" a couple of nights a week. Occasionally he took her out to dinner, but she understood that he didn't really want to be seen publicly with her. People who knew about Marjorie and knew him would "get the wrong idea." They couldn't know how much it meant to him just to spend time with her, talk about books, listen to music. It didn't occur to him, in the beginning, that it would be any more than that. She would give him a quick, friendly kiss on the cheek when he arrived. Moving about the kitchen, making drinks, tending to the record player, she would touch him in passing. Without really thinking, sitting at the table in the enchanted kitchen, sipping after-dinner coffee and brandy—which he had brought with him—he would find his hand resting on hers. She made no move to avoid it.

Some months after it had become a regular thing he found her in a highly emotional state one night. One of her sons, working somewhere in the Southwest, was in trouble. She was vague about the trouble, but the boy needed financial help. The boy had asked his father for it and had been turned down.

"I'd rather be shot than ask you, Andrew," Allegra said to him. "But would you consider endorsing a note for me at the bank? I'd pay it off each week out of my salary."

"How much?" he asked.

"Six hundred dollars," she said.

He laughed. It was a pleasure to be needed. Six hundred

dollars meant nothing to him. He took his checkbook out of his pocket and wrote her a check. "This way you won't have to pay interest," he said.

The world was lifted off her back, it seemed. She put her arms around him and kissed him on the mouth. For just an instant he felt her warm, sweet tongue searching for his. He pulled away, jarred to his heels. Suddenly desire surged over him. He wanted her.

He skipped a week of seeing her. Fantasies made it unsafe. At the end of the week there was an envelope for him at his office. In it was a ten-dollar bill and a note. "It may take forever at this rate, Andrew dear, but it's the best I can do at the moment."

He went to see her again, and it was as though she was unaware that anything had happened. There was the casual kiss on his cheek, the casual touch. But it was no longer casual for him. His whole body began to tremble each time it happened.

At night, in his lonely bed at home, he dreamed of what it could be like to hold Allegra, in his arms, to feel once more the joy that had been a part of his life. But he didn't want anything quick, a clock hanging over his head that would remind him that he must get back to Marjorie.

He put it to her. He was in love with her. Would she go somewhere with him for a few days, a weekend? His need for her was interfering with his work, with his political plans.

She sounded distressed. "I swore to myself, Andrew, that I'd never do to another woman what was done to me. I'd never have an affair with a married man."

"But Marjorie is different," he said. "You wouldn't be taking anything away from her. She—it isn't possible for her. And oh, God, Allegra, I need you so very much."

They talked about it, back and forth, and finally, miracle of miracles, she said she would go with him. But it would have to be the weekend after next.

10

He walked on air. He came every other night to see her, bringing gifts, bringing liquor. And he held his desires in check. He must wait for it to be just right.

Four days before the Friday they were to take off, he went to the cottage carrying brandy. Just four more days! He was absurdly gay, but Allegra seemed distant, distressed about something. She didn't unwrap the bottle, left it standing on the kitchen table.

"I have to tell you something, Andrew," she said. "I'd rather cut out my tongue than do it. But—I can't go through with our plan."

"Oh, God!" he said.

"It's better to hurt you now than later," she said. "It simply doesn't have the right chemistry for me. I might do it because I'm indebted to you for your friendship, your help. But I just couldn't make it good for you, make it what you want."

"Chemistry!" His voice choked in his throat.

"Dear Andrew, I'm so very, very sorry. I'm just not ready yet for anything—from you or anyone else."

He staggered out of the cottage to his car. He drove around the country side for hours, the wound unbearable. He wept with pity for himself.

Julian Quist had listened to this saga of an adolescent love affair between a fifty-six-year-old man and a forty-three-year-old woman, wondering what this had to do with running for the United States Senate. There must be more to come, he thought.

There were beads of sweat standing out on Andrew Crown's forehead. He blotted at them with a white linen handkerchief. His mouth was unsteady as he proceeded with his story. He was a man suffering from a deeper agony than his story, at least so far, warranted.

"You're probably thinking I'm just a dirty old man, out

for a sex fling with some available broad," Crown said. "I was in love with her, Julian, whatever that means. I wanted to spend all my free time with her. I wanted to give her everything I had to give, which was so damned little!" Crown seemed to find it hard to breathe, as though he'd been running. "I couldn't offer her marriage. I couldn't walk out on what is left of Marjorie, no matter how desperately I wanted Allegra. I had thought, if we went away somewhere for a few days, came fully together, that we'd be able to talk about some sort of future." A note of hysteria crept into Crown's short laugh. "But I didn't produce the right chemistry for her! God almighty! Well, I didn't go back, or call, or communicate in any way for two weeks. But I couldn't shake it— not for one single waking moment. She was always there, faintly in the background or focused, sharp and bright, in front of me. It was simply unthinkable, unacceptable, that I should lose her. So, night before last, I drove out to her cottage." Crown hesitated. "Eleven o'clock in the morning is a bit early in the day, Julian, but would you mind if I poured myself a drink?"

Quist waved toward the little chromium-trimmed bar in the corner of his office. He didn't speak. He didn't want to break the spell. What was coming was evidently what really mattered, what had brought this political man, this public man, to Quist with an intensely private story.

Crown poured himself a straight slug of bourbon and tossed it off, standing by the bar. Then he began to talk again, not moving, his face turned away from Quist.

"Daylight was almost gone when I got there. Allegra's car, a VW, was parked in front of the cottage. I noticed a woman in a wide straw hat working in a garden across the way. She didn't have much light left, I thought. Some one of the Braden clan. I almost ran to the door of the cottage. Somehow I had convinced myself that Allegra would greet me with pleasure, let me take her in my arms, make me the promise I wanted her to make.

"There was a small light burning in the kitchen, but no sign of her. I opened the door and stepped in, planning to call to her. I—I never did. Oh, God!"

"Something had happened to her?" Quist asked, speaking for the first time. He spoke because it seemed Crown couldn't go on.

"Something was happening to her!" Crown almost shouted. "Upstairs. The moans, the little cries of joy of a woman near to sexual climax. The activity—on the bed. I—I didn't have the right chemistry for her—but someone else did!"

Quist's jaw muscles tightened. Crown's pain was so unbearable he could almost feel it himself.

"I—I ran out of there," Crown said in a shaken voice. "I wanted to get away as fast as I could, as far as I could, to the end of the goddamned earth. As I—reached my car the woman who had been gardening called out to me. Could she help me? I—I shouted back at her. I'd been looking for Mrs. Landis but she wasn't at home, I said. The woman said, 'Well, that's her car.' I said Mrs. Landis must have gone somewhere with someone. And I got the hell out of there."

Crown turned back to the bar and poured himself another drink. When he didn't go on Quist asked him if that was all.

"All? Oh, God!" Crown said. He walked over to a window and stood looking down at the city. Then he turned and faced Quist, gripping the back of a chair for support. His eyes were burning. "I didn't sleep all night. I was obsessed by the ghastly vision of her in the arms of another man. I—I didn't go to the office the next morning. I drove round and round the countryside, trying to persuade myself I hadn't heard what I'd heard. She had castrated me, Julian, by turning to someone else. Last night I went to bed. I still couldn't sleep. There's a bedside radio in my room. I turned it on, hoping to distract myself. Then I heard it. 'Local police report

13

finding the naked body of Mrs. Allegra Landis floating in the pool back of her cottage. She had been stabbed several times in the chest and abdomen.' " Crown closed his eyes, fighting for control. "There was more, Julian. The report had it that Mrs. John Braden, whose husband rented Mrs. Landis her cottage, reported seeing a strange man leaving the cottage shortly before dark. This man had stated that Mrs. Landis wasn't at home. Mrs. Braden thought he seemed agitated, and he drove away in a great hurry. She wasn't able to describe him too exactly. 'But I'd know him if I saw him again,' she said."

"Oh, brother!" Quist said.

"So you see why I had to tell you this, Julian," Crown said. "I have to withdraw from the campaign. I can't let myself be photographed. I have to go into hiding until the police find out who—who killed her." He turned back to the window. "If I'd only called out to her! If I'd only made a disgusting scene, rushed up to the bedroom! She might be alive if I hadn't been such a delicate sonofabitch!"

CHAPTER TWO

Quist leaned forward and pressed a buzzer on his desk. Crown had turned back toward the bar. Connie Parmalee, Quist's secretary, stepped in from her own office. She was a tall girl, with copper-colored hair, a fine long-legged figure, a face almost Oriental in its bone structure, and gray-green eyes that were partially hidden by a pair of tinted granny-glasses.

"A woman named Mrs. Allegra Landis was murdered in

the town of Cranville, on the Island, night before last," Quist said to Connie. "Found naked in her pool, stabbed to death. Find out what the local press and the radio and TV stations have on it, Connie. New York papers must have it by now. Mrs. Landis's cottage is on the John Braden estate. He's a sportsman, horse fancier. He's enough of a celebrity so that a murder on his estate makes it something more than a local thing."

Connie's eyes moved from Quist to Andrew Crown's square shoulders at the bar, then back to Quist.

"If you have to talk to anyone, leave me out of it," Quist said. "Make it personal. The dead woman was a friend of yours."

Connie turned and walked out of the office. Two and two make four. She didn't have to ask questions. It was what made her a super-secretary.

Lying on Quist's desk was a manila folder. The tab on it read, simply, ANDREW CROWN. It was typical of Connie's efficiency that the moment Crown had been announced by the receptionist the Crown folder had been placed at Quist's elbow. He opened it now, frowning. The top sheet was a time schedule. Today was Wednesday. The following Monday, Crown was scheduled to announce his candidacy for the Senate, and the campaign would begin full blast. Dozens of details had been arranged for Monday; a public announcement of the Party's support; an appearance on the Today show; a press conference following a fancy luncheon for big shots at Willard's Back Yard.

Involvement in a murder before Monday could blow the ball game almost before it started. A great many thousands of dollars had been spent already on campaign literature, radio and TV time, activities that had led to the Party's support.

"We have a number of options, Andrew," Quist said,

breaking the silence in the office.

Crown turned slowly away from the bar. He looked old and beaten.

"We can delay the announcement."

"What reason would we give?" Crown asked in a dull voice. "It isn't exactly a secret except to the general public. And they've been given some pretty strong hints by the political commentators."

"Marjorie's health?" Quist suggested.

"No!" Crown almost shouted. He came toward Quist's desk. "I don't give a damn whether I run for office or not, Julian. I don't want Marjorie to know about Allegra. Use Marjorie as a public excuse and she'll know it's a lie. My problem is to keep Mrs. John Braden from identifying me as the man she saw leaving Allegra's cottage. If she does that, Marjorie will be certain I was unfaithful to her."

"And you were," Quist said. "You dreamed of it hundreds of times; you wanted it; you campaigned for it. How much more unfaithful would you have been if you'd had your weekend with the lady?"

"Damn you, Julian, it didn't happen!" Crown said. "Marjorie doesn't have to know about it now. She doesn't have to be hurt. I'm not going to let her be hurt. Are you my friend, or do I have to go somewhere else for help?"

Quist took a long, thin cigar from a humidor on his desk and lit it, eyes squinted against the smoke.

"I'm your friend, Andrew," he said finally.

Crown let out his breath in a long sigh. "Thanks, friend," he said. "I thought first of going to a private detective. But I couldn't tell him what I've told you. I couldn't explain why I want him to work on a case the police are handling. I can trust you to keep what I've told you a secret. No one else."

"If I'm to help you, there are some people who will have to know, Andrew."

"Who? And why, for God sake?"

"I have no secrets from Lydia," Quist said. "I'll need help from Dan Garvey and Bobby Hilliard. My secretary has already guessed."

"Oh, God!" Crown said.

Lydia Morton, dark, sultry, with a marvelous figure, looked more like a high fashion model than the brilliant writer and researcher she was. But she was much more than that to Quist. She spent most of her non-working time in Quist's Beekman Place apartment. They were as deeply in love as any two people could be. There were never any secrets from Lydia about anything. Dan Garvey, the dark opposite of Quist's golden blondness, once a star athlete, was a very good man to have in your corner when the going got tough. Bobby Hilliard, looking like a young Jimmy Stewart, handled temperamental clients with gentle skills. These three were the "associates" of Julian Quist Associates. No secrets from any of them—nor from Connie Parmalee, his secretary.

"They don't have to know anything if you walk out of here now and get your help somewhere else," Quist said. "If you're to get help from here it has to be all of us. None of them will talk, or gossip, or pass on a word. But they have to know why we're doing what we will do."

"I have to trust them," Crown said.

"Good. Knowing the whole truth, Andrew, we have leads the police don't have. We have four days before the big decision has to be made. We have to keep you away from cameras until someone comes up with the killer."

"How?"

"Just stay out of sight," Quist said. "Now for some questions that may be painful."

"Go," Crown said.

"Did you believe what Allegra told you about not being ready—for you or anyone else?"

"I believed. Until—"

"You heard her in the hay with someone."

17

"Yes."

"How do you account for it?"

Crown shrugged. It was a gesture of despair. "She was lying to me. I never went there before without calling her in advance."

"Did she ever turn you down when you suggested a visit?"

"I—I don't think so."

"So you don't think she was stringing you along?"

"What am I to think?"

"What about the husband?"

"She told me he was the only man she'd ever had sex with. Her first and her last."

"So, if he came back she might have given in to him?"

Crown's eyes widened. "I—I suppose so."

Quist's cigar had gone out and he relit it. "What about the husband's new wife?"

"Her name is Louise," Crown said, "but Allegra called her Red. She was, according to Allegra, a topless dancer in some joint in Cranville. An accomplished whore, Allegra called her."

"It's a starting point," Quist said. "Let me say this to you, Andrew. To have any hope of getting at what happened we're going to have to find out everything there is to know about your Allegra. The results may not be pleasant for you."

"If I was wrong about her," Crown said, "it might help to bear what's happened."

"What about the man she worked for? Did you say his name was Eliot Keyes?"

"He's a very good lawyer," Crown said. "Corporation law. Not married. About fifty. Good reputation."

"Could Allegra have charmed him?"

Crown shook his head slowly. "She was an attractive woman, Julian. But not a sex queen on the surface."

"But she told you every stud in Cranville was after her."

18

"Women who have been married and are suddenly free are always targets, aren't they? I—I don't know how other men reacted to her, Julian. I never saw her with any other man. Ours was a—a very private, almost secret kind of relationship." Crown sounded bitter. "I didn't have the right chemistry for her. I can't guess who might have had, or for whom she had it."

"The husband had it for twenty-five years—until he caught up with his topless redhead."

"I suppose."

"What about the Bradens?"

"Very social, from what Allegra told me. Endless parties. He is a top steeplechase rider. They train hunters there on the estate. I understand Allegra's cottage was built for their daughter. A sort of elaborate playhouse. But the daughter married and lives in Europe somewhere. The cottage was available to the right person, and Eliot Keyes persuaded the Bradens that Allegra was a 'right person.' "

"Allegra's sons?"

"The one I helped is somewhere in the Southwest—Texas, New Mexico. I never really cared, Julian. The other one is in the army, NATO forces in Europe."

"What other family?"

"None that she ever mentioned. I mean, both parents dead. She never mentioned any brothers or sisters."

Quist stood up and dropped his cigar in an ash tray. "Go home, Andrew. Stay out of sight. Make your peace with yourself if you can. I'll be in touch."

Connie Parmalee's preliminary report on Allegra Landis was short and uncolored. It was on Quist's desk when he came back from a hastily arranged luncheon with Lydia Morton and Dan Garvey. They were with him when he picked up the report and read it aloud to them. Lydia sat in one of the modern chrome-trimmed chairs, her elegant long

19

legs stretched out in front of her. Garvey stood by the windows, looking down at the helicopter landing pad on the roof of an adjoining building.

There had been disagreements at lunch. Garvey had been a star running back in college, and a brilliant pro-football career stretched out in front of him until it was cut short, overnight, by a knee injury. A highly competitive man used to meeting any challenge in a head-on-head test of strength, Garvey disliked the subtle and the devious. He thought Andrew Crown should go to the police, tell what he knew about that night, identify himself as the man Mrs. Braden had seen leaving the cottage and damn the torpedoes.

"My guess is it wouldn't hurt his election chances," Garvey had insisted over lunch. "Not half as much as it might hurt him later on, even with the killer caught, to have Mrs. Braden come out with an identification when she sees him on TV. Why hadn't he come forward? Much harder to answer that question later than now."

"You're overlooking a key element, Dan," Lydia had said. Lunch for Lydia was a vodka martini on the rocks, two slices of dry melba toast, decorated by a thin covering of Roquefort cheese.

"What key element?"

"Marjorie Crown. If he wades in, as you suggest, she has to know. I gather Crown would rather lose the ball game than have that happen."

"So he can't win," Garvey had said, impatient. "Sooner or later Mrs. Braden will point a finger at him."

"If we can serve up the real killer on a platter, the identification won't matter," Quist had said. "When Andrew isn't a murder suspect—which he would be right now—there can be a dozen reasonable explanations for his having been there that night. She was doing some extra secretarial work for him. Something like that. Mrs. Braden could, if she's a human being and not a harpie, agree to keep still about him."

"And if she's a Conservative and not a Party member?" Garvey had asked.

Lydia had sipped her martini. "If Marjorie Crown is the kind of woman she is supposed to have been before her accident, sensitive, alive, in love with Andrew, she'll know without being told. I'd know if you were interested in someone else, Julian, without anyone else to point a finger for me."

"You are a witch," Quist had said. "How could I even look at anyone else?"

"It's hard to be a witch in a wheelchair," Lydia had said, her dark eyes sad.

"God damn it, you're not a detective, Julian!" Garvey had exploded. "There's nothing that requires you to stick your neck out for a client."

"Andrew is more than a client. He's a friend," Quist had said.

"I go along with Julian," Lydia said then.

"I am, for God sake, always outvoted!" Garvey complained.

And then they had talked of ways and means. Now, back in the office, Quist read his friends Connie's report.

"ALLEGRA LANDIS, nee GRAVES: Born in New York City 1933. Parents Lawrence and Mathilda Graves. Lawrence Graves a successful and wealthy stockbroker, socially prominent, who went broke in the 1929 crash. Family moved to Cranville after Allegra's birth. Mathilda Graves died of cancer in 1938. Lawrence Graves, left with a little girl child, began to drink himself to death which he accomplished in 1942, not long after Pearl Harbor. A widow named Elaine Potter, a long-time friend, undertook to raise the child. When Allegra was seventeen she ran away with James Landis and married him. He was older, with a not-too-fragrant reputation. Gambling, particularly horses, a womanizer. But the marriage seemed to work. He settled down. Became the manager of a supermarket in Flushing. Gambling and women appeared to be forgotten. Allegra had two sons and several pregnancies that didn't work out. Her first son, Patrick, now 24, is a replica of his father in the early days—wild, undisciplined, took off for parts unknown after high school. Second son, David, now 22, quiet, studious, was taken into the army and is serving in NATO forces in Germany.

"Mrs. Potter saw to it that Allegra had a business education. Trained as a secretary. She did part-time work after her marriage for Walton Keyes, father of her present employer, Eliot Keyes. The Landis family seemed like a good one, Allegra and Jim Landis devoted. Suddenly, out of the blue, he took off with one Louise Stancyk, a part-time call girl and discotheque dancer. That was a little over a year ago. Note: He got the divorce, not Allegra. Grounds, extreme mental cruelty, which can mean anything. No question of custody of the boys. They were both of age. Allegra, with the help of Eliot Keyes, rented the cottage on the Braden place a little over a year ago.

"PRESENT SITUATION: Night before last Mrs. Braden saw a man leaving the cottage. He seemed agitated. He said he'd come to see Allegra but she was out. Mrs. Braden pointed out Allegra's car which was parked near the cottage and the man suggested she must have gone out with someone. It was almost dark so Mrs. Braden couldn't give too detailed a description of the man, who drove away. She had no reason to suspect anything, so she can't say what kind of car it was. Never thought of looking for a license plate number. But she thinks she'd know the man if she saw him again. The police have her going through mug shot books, looking for him there.

"Yesterday morning one of the Bradens' dogs, a Dalmatian if it matters, set up a barking and caterwauling and wouldn't come when called. John Braden went to see what the trouble was and came on Allegra's nude body floating in a small pool behind the cottage. The police report she died of multiple stab wounds.

"They say 'an arrest is expected soon,' but the fact is they have no solid lead; no fingerprints except Allegra's. Nothing that points to anyone at all—except Mrs. Braden's agitated man. They are pinning all their hopes on her being able to identify him. The County Prosecutor is in charge of the case. He is a man named George Spellman. There is a special investigator connected with Spellman's office named Henry Bonham. Of course there are the State Police and the local sheriff.

"From what I can gather in the short time I've had, boss, Allegra Landis was well liked in the community. People were shocked by the breakup of the marriage and most people say Jim Landis is a bastard. But may I remind you, he got the divorce. More as I can dig it up. CP."

Quist looked up at Lydia and Garvey. "Some puzzling contradictions, wouldn't you say?"

Garvey turned away from his inspection of the helicopter pad. "Does it occur to you, Julian, that every word your friend Crown told you may be true, but that he stopped before the end of the story?"

"Meaning?"

"That he went back to the cottage later and butchered his lady love?"

"Oh, no," Lydia said.

"Waited for her lover to leave and polished her off. Now he wants you to clear him."

"So who was that lover?" Quist said. "Who was the man she was prepared for and took on so eagerly? The police aren't looking for him. They don't know about him."

"And he hasn't come forward," Lydia said.

"Neither would I if I were in his shoes," Garvey said. "I

23

don't like the smell of it, Julian."

"We have four days," Quist said. "Let's see what we can do with them."

There is something about a strange place, Quist thought, when you know something sinister has happened there. Things take on an aura of evil; people look secretive and fearful; the shadows are darker; voices sound threatening. And the whole thing is nonsense.

Cranville, on the Island, is like a lot of small towns in an expanding suburbia. There is a main highway, four to six lanes wide, running through an alley of gas stations, gift shops, garages, eating places, decorated after dark by garish neon signs. You can stop anywhere and buy anything that suits you, provided it is tasteless. You wonder, if you are driving through, how people can live in such a junk yard of tourist traps. But if you turn off the highway at an inconspicuous, almost invisible sign that says, for example, VILLAGE OF CRANVILLE—1 MILE, the garishness is suddenly gone and you get an entirely different image of what the people of this community are like and how they live.

Two windblown people in a Mercedes convertible found the turnoff to Cranville on Thursday morning of the week Allegra Landis was murdered. Quist at the wheel, looking like a Greek god on an ancient coin with his golden hair rumpled, found himself thinking that, except for the occasional thunder of an airplane overhead, the modern world had passed Cranville by. It must look very much as it had fifty years ago except that the roads were black-topped where they had once been carefully graded gravel. The graceful trees surrounding the village green were older, of course, but the houses, even the places of business, had the elegance, the patina, of age. Houses had dates on them going back to Revolutionary times. Approaching the center of the village Quist had noticed many gateways leading to hidden homes.

A cool breeze with a salty tang to it reminded him that they were not far from the ocean.

"This place smells of money," Quist said to Lydia, who was slumped down in the seat beside him.

"I can't get it out of my head that it smells of death," Lydia said. Her dark eyes were hidden by a pair of black, wire-rimmed glasses.

Along with Garvey and Bobby Hilliard they had planned a game of cat-and-mouse to play for the next few days. They couldn't barge into Cranville and start asking questions without attracting attention from the wrong people—the County Prosecutor and the Special Investigator. Very shortly after that happened someone would come up with the information that Julian Quist Associates were about to handle a political campaign for Andrew Crown. Once that was mentioned, Mrs. John Braden—Nancy Braden—might remember that she had seen Crown somewhere and that he was the agitated man who'd left Allegra's cottage the night of the murder. Crown had mentioned that he didn't know the Bradens, but he was a local lawyer, a prominent citizen, and, reminded of him, Nancy Braden's memories might click into place.

The offices of Eliot Keyes, the lawyer for whom Allegra had worked, were located in a graceful old Colonial house on the green. No office buildings in Cranville. "Keyes has the keys to the problem," Bobby Hilliard had said, with his Jimmy Stewart grin. Nobody had thought it was funny at the time. The gambit wasn't complicated. They would approach Keyes with something totally unrelated to the murder. It would appear to be normal curiosity if they got around to talking about the murder of his girl Friday.

A middle-aged, matronly woman with a pleasant professional smile greeted Quist and Lydia in the entrance hall of the elegant old house. She was afraid Keyes couldn't see them this morning. He was just about to take off for the funeral of an employee.

Lydia, who had taken off the black glasses, batted her long eyelashes at the receptionist whose name, according to a plaque on her desk, was MRS. MOFFET. "The secretary who was killed?"

It was ghoulish, Quist said later, laughing.

"Poor Allegra," Mrs. Moffet said. She looked as if she was about to burst into tears on the spot.

"If Mr. Keyes could give me five minutes I could at least alert him to what I hope he will undertake for me," Quist said. "If he's interested, then I could come back another time."

Mrs. Moffet, sniffling, went off to ask.

"The lady may be a gold mine," Quist said to Lydia. "Stay with her while I talk to Keyes. Gossip, love. Gossip!"

Mrs. Moffet returned, followed by a rather handsome elderly man wearing a dark suit, a white shirt, with a black knit tie. Dark hair was graying at the temples. Man of distinction, Quist thought.

"I can only give you a very few minutes, Mr. Quist," Keyes said. He had a deep, musical voice. He must be very impressive in a courtroom. "I believe Mrs. Moffet has explained to you—?"

"A ghastly business," Quist said.

He followed Keyes down the carpeted hallway to the lawyer's private office. It was a paneled room, with bookcases filled with a calf-bound law library plus other important-looking books. Except for the books it was more of a comfortable consulting room than an office. Flowers in a vase on the desk.

"Coffee?" Mr. Keyes asked. There was an electric coffee maker on a table behind his desk.

"I won't hold you up that long," Quist said.

Keyes waved toward a deep, brown leather armchair. "I know you by reputation, Mr. Quist. You promoted the Island Arena, helped with the fund raising. The communities on this part of the Island and the millions of sports fans within range of the Arena should be grateful to you for the first-rate job you did."

Quist gave him a relaxed smile. "I should get you to write a testimonial for me for future clients," he said.

"The Arena is all the testimonial you need, Mr. Quist."

Quist saw that his man was politely impatient. "It's about my connection with the Arena that I came to see you, Mr. Keyes."

"Oh?"

It came easily, "trippingly on the tongue." "My connection with the Arena didn't end with the completion of the building. Julian Quist Associates has a long-term contract to promote its activities. There are decisions, and sometimes contracts, that need immediate handling. Neither I nor our lawyer can come out here every time there is a question. I want to find a resident stand-in I can trust."

"Let me think," Keyes said. "The Arena already has an attorney—Andrew Crown. Friend of mine."

"I know Andrew well," Quist said. "But he works for the Arena corporation. I want someone to represent me."

"Maybe I can think of someone," Keyes said.

"Oh, I've already thought of someone. You, Mr. Keyes. I'd like you to be my representative—on the spot. If we can agree on a retainer—?"

"How did you happen to choose me?" Keyes asked.

Quist gave him what he hoped was a sly look. "Oh, I made some inquiries, Mr. Keyes. If you're willing to consider it, perhaps we could set up a date, preferably in my office where all the records and contracts are kept, and we can go over the details—and discuss a retainer."

"I'd be interested," Keyes said. "The first of next week?"

"A difficult time for me," Quist said. "We're launching a

27

new promotion then." He didn't add "I hope!" "I *could* come out here tomorrow or the next day if that would be more convenient."

Keyes frowned. "It would be helpful to me. I have something of a problem here. As Mrs. Moffet told you, I believe, I'm on my way now to the funeral of a woman who has been my secretary for more than a year and a part-time employee for many years. Her death has left things here in the office in a state of some confusion."

Quist sighed. They had gotten around the main corner. "The woman who was murdered?" he asked, quite casual. "I saw an account in yesterday's *Daily News.*"

"Shocking and very distressing to me," Keyes said. "Allegra Graves worked for my father more than twenty-five years ago. When she married a man named Landis, she left us to raise a family. But she came here from time to time to help us out. A first-class secretary, a first-rate woman. A little more than a year ago she and her husband were divorced. It was very rough for her. Fortunately it coincided with my need for someone full time. First-class secretaries have a way of getting married just when they have become indispensable. Allegra was able to fill a gap for me. Now this—" He was clearly feeling a personal loss.

"The story in the paper wasn't very detailed," Quist said. If Keyes would talk he was there to listen.

"Beyond the fact that she was raped and brutally stabbed to death, the police don't have much. They're looking for a man Mrs. Braden saw leaving the cottage that night, but she can't give much of a description and the man hasn't come forward." Keyes' mouth tightened into a thin, straight line. "When they catch the man who did it, I'd like to be the prosecutor. And I could wish the Supreme Court hadn't been so tender-minded about the death penalty."

"The ex-husband; were he and Mrs. Landis on friendly terms?"

"They were *not!* And in my book Jim Landis is a bastard! I'd wonder about him but he has an unbreakable alibi for that night. He—" Keyes hesitated, his eyes widening. "Now that's a coincidence, Mr. Quist. Jim Landis works at the Island Arena. I believe he manages the food concessions there. In any case the circus is at the Arena, as you probably know. Landis was on the job for the evening performance, but after that he stayed all night to provide food and other supplies to the circus attendants who had to be there with the animals. He was alibied for the whole night. Well, I must be getting on, Mr. Quist. You name the time for tomorrow or Friday and I'll make it fit my plans."

"Can I call you first thing in the morning?"

"Fine."

Eliot Keyes was not a man to leave loose ends or have false innuendos be a part of his life. At the door he turned to Quist.

"As you gather, I dislike Jim Landis intensely," he said. "But I don't want to leave you with the inference that I suspect him of this brutal business. His alibi appears to be solid, but beyond that, Mrs. Braden knows him. He wasn't the man she saw at the cottage nor did he resemble him in any way. That man was short and stocky. Landis is tall with a magnificent body for a man of fifty-odd. He's a physical culture nut. I hadn't meant you to think—"

Quist smiled at him. "I hadn't really given it any thought at all," he said. He remembered, with gratitude, his grandmother telling him that white lies would probably be forgiven in heaven.

"Whatever you do, never hire Mrs. Moffet to work for you," Lydia said, as she and Quist drove slowly along the village green. "There are no secrets from that lady, and I suspect that if she didn't know anything about you she'd invent something."

"Perhaps that's why Keyes hired Allegra Landis when he

needed a new secretary instead of promoting Mrs. Moffet."

Lydia laughed. "Women are the doormats of the world. The slaves and sex objects of some kind of slavering male monsters. 'My husband was an animal! I was degraded and made use of all of our married life.' "

"And you said that you, too, found yourself constantly subjected to the degrading attacks of males?" Quist suggested.

"I did, may God forgive me," Lydia said. "But please, Julian, don't let it be any other way."

"A promise," Quist said. "What did your perfidy get you?"

"It got me 'poor Allegra,' " Lydia said, amusement fading from her eyes. "As soon as 'poor Allegra' was divorced, she found herself, like Mrs. Moffet when she was widowed, a target for all the males, attached or unattached, in the town. They assume, according to Mrs. Moffet, that you are deprived, starved for sex. That they are doing you a kindness by offering to brutalize you. 'Poor Allegra' was, you might say, in shock after her divorce. She had thought her marriage a total success, in all ways. Then that miserable Jim Landis had run off with a go-go dancer. Mrs. Moffet didn't mention the topless aspects of it. Sex with anyone else was unthinkable to 'poor Allegra.' Yet she was propositioned every day of her life, according to Mrs. Moffet. When it was learned that she was living alone in that cottage on the Braden place, all kinds of men appeared at all hours of the night wanting to force themselves on her. In the end, according to Mrs. Moffet, 'poor Allegra' had to lock and bar her door."

"You say 'poor Allegra' with something that sounds like bitterness," Quist said.

Lydia laughed again. "Envy," she said. "To hear Mrs. Moffet tell it, Allegra was the most wanted woman in the United States."

"Only it appears she didn't want to be wanted," Quist said.

"You're forgetting the little moans and cries of joy that Andrew Crown heard. Of course I want to be wanted! The fact that I limit my availability to you doesn't make being wanted by someone else any less gratifying."

Quist grinned at her. "I prefer to discuss the eccentricities of 'poor Allegra,' " he said. "Was there any discussion of Jim Landis? I still find myself interested in him, in spite of his perfect alibi and the fact that he wasn't the agitated man Mrs. Braden saw."

"According to Mrs. Moffet he is a monster, a betrayer, a lover of loose women," Lydia said.

Quist pulled the Mercedes over to the side of the road, into the shade of an ancient maple tree. He sat staring straight ahead, frowning. Lydia watched him, waiting for his next lead. She knew this stop meant that something was percolating with him. They knew each other so well that she sensed exactly what he hoped for from her. In this case, silence.

"On the surface," Quist said finally, "the facts would seem to contradict Andrew Crown's concept of Allegra," he said. "She wasn't ready for him or anyone else, she told Andrew. Yet she had open arms for someone. This suggests she had just been playing Andrew for fish. She got some money from him."

"Not much in Andrew's terms," Lydia said. "And she was paying it back, ten bucks a week. Not very sinister."

"If she didn't care for him, wasn't pleased with his company, why should she have wanted to string him along?" Quist asked.

"She was like me," Lydia suggested. "She liked to be wanted but she wasn't available."

"Yet she told Andrew she'd go away with him for a weekend."

"Not because she wanted him, but because he wanted her so badly and he was such a nice guy with deep troubles. But then she played it honest. It didn't have the right 'chemistry' for her. One weekend she might have gone for. But she knew Andrew wouldn't let it rest there. Better to hurt him now than later, when he'd want it even more."

"You're defending her," Quist said.

"Devil's advocate. I'm just laying out one possible story. As you say, why string Andrew along?"

"Some women revel in teasing men," Quist said.

Lydia's smile was one-sided. "You know that from experience?"

"I'm not teasable," Quist said. "Andrew, on the other hand, is. He was full of guilts about Marjorie. He was willing to be delayed. I imagine he subconsciously hoped Allegra would say no. It would save him from hurting Marjorie. But when she said yes the dam burst. Then she said no—the teasing technique—and there was no turning back for him."

"And he found her having a good, healthy romp in the hay."

"Can you make that fit in with the idea that she was a nice, non-teasing woman?" Quist asked.

"Of course," Lydia said. "She had spent twenty-five years in one bed with one man. There was never anyone else. He was completely satisfactory for her, and she supposed she was all he wanted. Then he lowers the boom. That's a lot tougher to take than the 'no' she gave Andrew. If you walked out on me, Julian, with another woman, it would be a long time before my self-confidence was restored enough for me to take on someone else. And if you came back—"

"I would come back," Quist said, smiling at her.

"So you would come back, ask me to forgive you, ask me to forget, and, God help me, I'd say yes, and I'd be in your bed before you could say—Jim Landis!"

"You think that's what happened?"

"It could have," Lydia said, "and it would leave her integrity intact. Landis comes to see her. The topless tootsie turns out to have been a mistake. He wants forgiveness. He wants

32

back in. Isn't he the only man she'd ever had, ever wanted? The sounds of joy that Andrew heard could have been real joy, not just a sexual moment. Her world was restored."

"So then the prodigal husband stabs her in the chest, the stomach, dumps her in the pool and goes back to the topless tootsie. Why?"

"Maybe he didn't. Maybe he went home to break things off with the topless tootsie."

"You're not forgetting that Keyes says he has an alibi for the whole evening," Quist said.

"If I were investigating this case, I'd want to check that alibi for myself," Lydia said. "Let's say, for the moment, he was at the cottage, made love to a more than willing Allegra, and took off. What do we have? We have Andrew Crown who heard it all and is—he says—wandering around eating his heart out. As Dan said, he could have left out the part about going back to the cottage after husband-lover had left, and punished her permanently for having betrayed him. Or —Topless Tootsie could have followed her man to the cottage, known what was happening, waited for Landis to leave and then carved up Allegra. Woman scorned. Then there is Charlie Spivak."

"Who the hell is Charlie Spivak?" Quist asked.

"According to Mrs. Moffet, Charlie Spivak is known locally as the Cranville Stud. He is one of the people against whom Allegra is supposed to have locked and barred her door. Backdoor gossip has everyone in the village laughing at Charlie Spivak. Nobody has been known to have said 'no' to him before Allegra."

"So?"

"So the Cranville Stud goes to the cottage to try again. He finds the lady in the hay with someone else. He waits for that someone to leave. Then he takes his shattered ego into the cottage, is turned down once more, and punishes Allegra for having had the gall to refuse him."

Quist shook his head. "You're amazing, Lydia," he said.

"I know," she said demurely.

"Do you often dream up fantasies like this?"

"About other people, not us," Lydia said.

"There could be something to the general theory—that Landis was the man in Allegra's bed and someone punished her for it. How do we find out?"

" 'Ask the man who owns one,' " Lydia said. "Jim Landis has all the answers. There must be some way to get him to talk."

"I think there may be," Quist said after a moment.

CHAPTER THREE

There was a time, perhaps incredible to the younger generations, when spectator sports were played outdoors. You went to a big league baseball game in the afternoon, and you sat in the sun. You went to football games, college or professional, in the afternoon, dressed for whatever the weather might be. When night baseball was introduced in the thirties, people thought it was just a publicity gimmick. It wouldn't last—like the automobile! Now, eighty or ninety percent of all sporting events are not only played at night, but, more and more, they are being played undercover. Examples are the Houston Astrodome, the new complex in Pontiac, Michigan, where Detroit teams play their games, and the Island Arena. The Island Arena had been the dream of a group of men who planned the greatest sports complex in the world. It was big enough for baseball or football or soccer; it could house the circus; it could accommodate monster conventions, championship fights, hockey, basketball.

"And perfect if we revive an interest in the Christians versus the lions," Quist had remarked when he first saw the plans.

Access to the Arena was perfect. The Long Island Railroad stopped by one entrance; there were acres and acres of parking area that opened off the Island Thruways, engineered to eliminate traffic jams. There was even a marina to which you could come by boat, if you chose to be that exclusive.

There was only one problem connected with this "fabulous playpen," as Quist had called it. The costs of operating and maintaining it were so enormous that events had to be scheduled every day and every night of the year or the promoters would quickly find themselves drowning in a sea of red ink.

It was the job of Julian Quist Associates to keep a spotlight trained on the Arena. Not just locally. That was for the press and advertising departments. Exposure was needed all over the country, Canada, Mexico, the Caribbean Islands. In a political year there had been a dog-eat-dog battle for party conventions. The Arena was Dan Garvey's account, but there were red carpets rolled out for Quist and Lydia that Thursday afternoon.

Ted Frost, a very bright, very mod young man, was the General Manager of the Arena. Frost was Garvey's boy, a former flanker back in the National Football League who could run the 100 in 9.4 in a football uniform. He was a cheerful, bright, hard-driving optimist. He knew very well that no matter how pressed he was for time—and he was always pressed for time—Quist had to be catered to. Frost was Garvey's boy, and Garvey was Quist's boy. He wondered what the hell Quist was doing out here on a midweek afternoon. But "his not to reason why, his but to do and die."

The appearance of Lydia with Quist removed any vestige of irritation Frost had felt about having to interrupt his routines. Frost thought he had never seen quite such a tempting dish. He would be content to look her over forever—or at least until he could plan a flanking attack for himself. Frost's office was walled with pictures: athletes, actors, musicians, politicians, celebrities from all over the world.

Was it too early for a drink? Too bad. And was this a sightseeing tour or was Quist here for a specific purpose? The key to the city was his.

"I stumbled across something this morning that gives me mild concern," Quist said.

"Name it and we'll take care of it," Frost said, never taking his eyes off Lydia. If she was aware of his hot, hungry interest, she gave no sign of it.

"A man named James Landis," Quist said.

"Oh, wow! Poor bastard," Frost said. "You're thinking of what happened to his ex-wife?"

"I believe her funeral was this morning," Quist said.

"Who knows? Who cares?" Frost said. "As ye sow, so shall ye reap. Is that how it goes?"

"Biblical, but how does it apply to Mrs. Landis?" Quist asked, his face expressionless.

"The ex-Mrs. Landis," Frost said. "The present Mrs. Landis is something of a doll." His look at Lydia said "not so much of a doll as you, doll."

"You know something, Frost, or are you just repeating gossip?" Quist asked.

"Gossip," Frost admitted. "I understood the lady was available, but she was a little long in the tooth for me. But what has that got to do with the price of eggs? I mean, why are you concerned about the Landises?"

"A murder case doesn't help a public image," Quist said. "Oh, people will read about it. Unfortunately they will remember it. A consequential employee of the Island Arena is a murder suspect. It doesn't do us any good, Frost."

"Suspect?" Frost actually looked away from Lydia. "I

36

know the police questioned him, but I understood he was in the clear."

"That's what I want to make sure of," Quist says. "If he isn't, I think we should consider getting rid of him, or at least suspending him until the case is solved."

"That's asking him to prove his innocence before anyone has suggested he's guilty," Frost said.

Score one for Mr. Frost, Quist thought. That at least was a decent attitude. "Are you satisfied that he's innocent?"

"He has a perfect alibi, as I understand it," Frost said. "He was here from late afternoon till early morning. Some fourteen hours. We have a special problem with the circus. Their people don't go home after the evening performance, like a hockey team. There are at least a couple of hundred keepers, trainers, grips who have to bed down where the show is. They need food, coffee, beer, what have you, round the clock. That's Landis's department."

Quist took one of his long, thin cigars from his breast pocket and lit it. His eyes were narrowed against the smoke. "I'd guess it's only about a ten-minute drive from the Arena to the cottage where Allegra Landis was killed," he said. "Ten minutes to get there, ten minutes to kill her and dump her body in the pool, ten minutes to get back. Is his alibi so tight that there wasn't a half hour, forty minutes, unaccounted for—if someone tried to check?"

"Henry Bonham, the special investigator, was satisfied," Frost said. "I have an instinct for people, Mr. Quist. Part of my job. Jim Landis smells clean to me. He isn't a suspect, as far as I know."

Lydia looked up from under her long lashes. "I'm interested in the lady," she said. "Gossip told you she was available, Mr. Frost?"

He gave her an engaging smile. "A lot of men are pretty rotten about women," he said. "They like to boast about their conquests. It publicizes their manhood, if it needs advertising. At least a half dozen guys suggested, in my hearing, that Allegra baby had assumed the horizontal position for them. And that she was pretty hot stuff."

"Was Landis still attracted to her?" Lydia asked.

Frost laughed. "You haven't met Red Landis, the new wife," he said. "I gather getting the divorce from Allegra baby was the happiest day of his life. He got the divorce, you know. The grounds were extreme cruelty, or something like that. But I suspect Landis was just being polite. He must have come home some night and found her in bed with one of the Bradens' stableboys."

"But you don't know that for a fact?" Quist asked. He had decided Ted Frost was a little too glib for his taste.

"No. But something like that, I suspect."

"I think I'd like to talk to Landis," Quist said. "I'd like him to reassure me himself."

Frost looked boyishly helpless. "There's no way to account for some people's behavior," he said. "Landis took the day off to go to his ex-wife's funeral. I think he's pretty badly thrown by what happened to her. Even though they'd agreed to disagree, whatever she did to him, she was the mother of his two boys."

"When will he check back in?"

"Tonight, before the circus rolls."

"I think we'll come back to see him," Quist said.

"And so we seem to have two Allegras," Quist said, as he and Lydia drove away from the Arena. "The one who wasn't ready for any man, who'd never had sex with anyone but her lost husband, and the Allegra who was ready for anyone and had men by the carload. You pays your money and you takes your choice. How about you, ma'am? Which one do you buy?"

Lydia was wearing the black glasses again. The afternoon

sun was very bright. The glasses hid whatever her eyes might have revealed, but the corners of her mouth moved in a small smile.

"Did you notice the eye young Mr. Frost was giving me?" she asked.

"To change the subject, yes, I noticed the eye young Mr. Frost was giving you," Quist said. "I am quite accustomed to noticing the eye that all men give you, luv. But what has that to do with the two Allegras?"

"There are many ways that men look at women," Lydia said.

"Who should know better than you?" Quist said.

"There are two principal ways, however," Lydia said. "Reasonably well-adjusted men, like you, sweet, look at an attractive woman, appreciate the way she's turned out, her style, her figure, the energy she gives off. But you leave her her privacy."

"I don't follow—if you want me to," Quist said.

"The second way is young Mr. Frost's way of looking," Lydia said. "If you were to turn around and go back to his office and ask him what I'm wearing, he couldn't tell you. The minute I walked into his office he undressed me. I was stark naked the entire time I was there. He was fantasizing what he might do to me—or, to give him a break, what he might do *with* me. And tomorrow, Julian, if he should see me 'across a crowded room' he would turn to one of his male friends and imply that I am a conquest of his."

"At which point I wash out his mouth with soap," Quist said. "But," he repeated patiently, "what has that to do with the two Allegras?"

"Andrew Crown told you that after her divorce Allegra found herself a target. Mrs. Moffet confirmed that. Maybe she was telling a truth when she implied that all unattached women are targets. Allegra may have said 'no' quite pleasantly and unstuffily a hundred times. But there will always be the Ted Frosts who can't afford to let their friends think they may have failed. And so rumor grows, gossip spreads, and more young men make passes at Allegra, the 'available' divorcée, presumably hungering for that supposedly incomparable male gift, a romp in the hay. Thanks to the Ted Frosts of this world, Julian, the second Allegra, taking on the whole town, could be pure illusion. The gossip could be only what the Ted Frosts wish was true. If the real Allegra Landis will step forward, she could very well be the one-man woman Andrew Crown described."

Quist grinned at her. "A romp in the hay is not an incomparable gift?"

"It's not a gift at all. It is either a shared experience or it's a colossal bore," Lydia said.

"I love you for so many reasons," Quist said.

"Thank you, sir. I still go for Andrew Crown's Allegra. Andrew admitted failure, which is more likely to be the truth than a crowing over success. Where, by the way, are we headed?"

"The scene of the crime," Quist said.

There were stone gates with a name sign in a wrought-iron holder indicating that this was the entrance to the home of John W. Braden. Then there was a gently curving bluestone driveway, winding through a carefully cared-for stretch of woods. The wild flowers growing up around the trees had a rather formal look to them, not as though they'd "just happened" to grow there. After what seemed about three-quarters of a mile Quist's Mercedes came out into a lovely stretch of pasture land, fenced fields, and dozens of horses grazing, many of them now with lovely heads raised, ears pricked forward to attention, as the car moved on.

"Now you've got to admit this smells of money," Quist said.

"I admit," Lydia said. "God, aren't those horses beautiful!"

"You're probably looking at about a million dollars' worth," Quist said. "Rooster Braden would own nothing but the very best."

"Rooster?"

"Nickname," Quist said. "Short for Bantam Rooster, I suspect. This man is what is called a gentleman rider, luv. It means he doesn't get paid for doing his thing, which is riding in steeplechase races everywhere: Belmont, Aqueduct, Saratoga, Ireland, the British Grand National. Anywhere there's glory."

"But a little man, I gather. Bantam Rooster."

"Good riders are not often big men," Quist said. "Weight is a factor. But I've seen Rooster Braden ride. He's a little man made of steel. And crazy enough to risk his neck any race-day afternoon just for the sport of it. 'Guts of a burglar' they say about him at the Tracks." He gave Lydia a quick, sidewise glance. "Little men like Rooster Braden have a special kind of egomania. You may find him a new experience."

The road turned up a little rise and there was a new panorama. There were elaborate stables, built of fieldstone, small fenced-in paddocks, a large riding ring where there was current activity. And in the distance, on the highest piece of ground, a great stone house looked out over the dunes to the ocean.

"Money, money, money," Lydia said, sounding awed. "How did the Rooster make it?"

"He didn't," Quist said. "The lady who saw an agitated man leaving Allegra's cottage, Nancy Braden, was a Caldwell. The Caldwells are oil. Oil is money. When Rooster Braden married Nancy Caldwell, he was assured of everything he'd ever wanted in life. Everything that relates to horses, that is."

"Meaning what? What is he lacking?"

Quist shrugged. "Who knows what a man wants that money can't buy?" he said.

They came closer to the stables and the riding ring. In the ring a man wearing a turtleneck black shirt, tan jodhpurs, and a sort of white plastic crash helmet was mounted on a beautiful chestnut mare. The horse's neck was flecked with lather, nostrils flared. As they cantered down the ring Lydia thought the man and the horse were all one piece.

Three men who looked like stable hands hung over the rail of the ring. Beside them a Dalmatian dog sat, his head turned toward Quist and Lydia in the Mercedes, tail wagging excitedly. But the dog didn't move.

In the ring the rider turned his horse and headed him toward a high three-rail fence at the far end of the ring. The canter became a gallop and horse and rider thundered down on the jump. A few yards from it the rider lashed at the horse with his crop and shouted "Now! Now!" The perfect coordination of man and horse seemed to break. The horse lowered her head, shied, stopped dead. A less skillful rider would have shot over her head. But this man had been ready. They could hear the steady string of profanity as he jerked the horse's head around, lashed at its flanks again with his crop and started back down the ring.

Lydia's hand closed over Quist's. "Cruel!" she said.

"That's the Rooster," Quist said, his pale eyes narrowed.

Rooster Braden had turned his mount and once more they thundered down on the jump. Once more the man lashed at the horse with his crop and shouted "Now! Now!"

This time something almost breathtaking took place. The horse took off, sailing over the jump. The landing was perfect. Braden brought her to a stop, leaned forward, patting her neck. Then he slipped off, went to the mare's head, nuzzled his face against her nose, crooning at her like a mother to a favorite child.

"That's it, baby. That's it," they heard him say.

From the pocket of his jodhpurs he produced, of all things, a carrot. He fed it to the mare, who seemed happy and pleased with herself. Braden kept talking to her, patting her.

Two of the stablemen climbed over the fence into the ring. One of them was carrying a cooling blanket. He unfastened the saddle girth, took off the saddle, and covered the horse with a blanket. The second man had moved to the horse's head and took over from Braden. Braden gave the horse a final pat on the neck and then started walking toward the Mercedes which was parked just outside the ring. He was, Lydia thought, not more than five feet six or seven. He moved with extraordinary grace. He took off his plastic helmet as he approached, and sunlight reflected on shiny, raven-black hair. His forearms and hands were tanned a nut brown, and they looked powerful. He reached the fence, stepped up on the lowest rung, and leaned his forearms on the top rail. His smile was very white, slightly crooked. But it was his eyes that held Lydia. They were black, abnormally bright, eager as if he was searching for excitement.

"She's going to be a good one," he said.

"She's beautiful," Lydia said, looking at the mare who was being led out of the ring by the grooms.

"I caught a glimpse of you as I turned to make that second run," Braden said. "You thought I was being cruel. By the way, do I know you?"

"My name is Julian Quist," Quist said. "This is Miss Morton."

"Isn't that rather old-fashioned?" Braden asked, his smile widening.

"I don't follow," Quist said.

Braden's bright eyes were on Lydia. "In this day and age

to be called 'Miss' is old-fashioned, isn't it? It should be Miz, or Ms. I rather like it though. It makes it quite clear what your status is."

"I very much doubt that," Lydia said.

Braden looked away from Lydia, reluctantly. "Quist," he said. "Aren't you the public relations man for the Arena?"

"Bingo," Quist said.

There was a whimpering sound and Braden turned. The Dalmatian sat where he had been from the beginning, his tail now frantic.

"He stays where I tell him to stay," Braden said. "I have to keep him out of the ring when I'm schooling a horse. At ease, Hector."

The dog leaped up from his sitting position, ran to Braden, licked his hand, then turned his attention to Lydia.

"Hector!"

"I don't mind him," Lydia said. "I'm fond of dogs."

"If you pet him, he'll be all over you, Miss Morton." He climbed over the fence and dropped down beside the car. "I'm really not cruel to animals, Miss Morton. But when you're training a jumper the horse has to know who's boss. I've been working with Golden Belle for a week, trying to teach her to take off sooner. She had to get the message or it might be her neck and mine. At last she got it."

"Is Hector the dog who found the lady who was murdered here?" Quist asked. Hector had turned to him for attention and he was scratching the dog's ears.

Braden scowled. "Nasty business," he said. "I usually work my horses in the early morning. Cooler. Better time. But today I went to Allegra's funeral, which is why I was working Golden Belle this afternoon. Hell of a thing. You die, and nobody gives a damn. Where were her friends? Only ghouls, newspaper people, and an old lady who brought her up. And me."

"I believe her ex-husband was there," Quist said. "They

told me at the Arena he was there."

"Maybe. I would know him by sight. Never met him. Well, what can I do for you, Mr. Quist—and Miss Morton?"

"I wanted to talk to you about holding an international jumping contest at the Arena," Quist said blandly. "Teams and riders from all over the world. The general public doesn't understand the niceties of a horse show, but they love the competition of jumping events. They can see what's happening. They don't have to be aficionados. I thought of perhaps a week of competition between international teams and individuals." Quist smiled. "But we'd have to begin by lining up the very best, especially when that very best is a neighbor. Meaning you, Mr. Braden."

Braden grinned. "Flattery may get you someplace," he said. The bright eyes turned to Lydia again. "Is it too early in the day for a drink? There are endless details, pros and cons, to discuss about your idea, Quist. Give me a lift up to the house and we can toss it around."

"Sounds very pleasant," Quist said. "Hop in."

"You mind Hector?" Braden asked.

"Of course not."

Braden opened the door and he and the Dalmatian got into the rear seat of the car. "Take the next fork to the left," he said.

They moved off at a leisurely speed. They'd only gone a hundred yards past the stables when they saw what had to be Allegra Landis's enchanted cottage. It was set back in the shade of a cluster of ancient oaks and maple trees. There were the wisteria vines Andrew Crown had described.

"Is that where it—it happened?" Lydia asked.

"The scene of the crime," Braden said cheerfully. "Do I detect a special interest?"

"Most women react rather strongly to violence," Lydia said. "What was she like?"

"Allegra?"

In the rear-view mirror Lydia saw Braden's face transformed by a dark frown. He took a cigarette out of the breast pocket of his black shirt and lit it with a gold lighter. There was something so cold and hard about this little man that she felt a chill sweep over her. Instinct told her there was something dangerous about him. She felt Quist's hand rest reassuringly on her knee for an instant. Julian never missed atmospheric changes, she thought.

"Nancy, my wife, and I scarcely knew her," Braden said. "She was recommended to us as a tenant by a lawyer friend, Eliot Keyes. The cottage was built for my daughter, but she's married and gone to live in Ireland."

"You don't look old enough to have a married daughter," Quist said.

The clouds lifted. The bright smile was back on Braden's face. "The best, you say. Young, you say. Don't press your luck, Quist. I might get to suspect there was a design to your flattery."

"Of course there's a design," Quist said. "I want some information from you."

"Fair enough," Braden said.

"Was there a traffic in lovers at the cottage?" Quist asked.

"I honestly don't know," Braden said. "We had Allegra for cocktails the first day she moved in. She was pleasant, agreeable, but we didn't have much in common. She—she didn't know one end of a horse from the other. She had a job with Keyes, was away all day, weekdays. She made it fairly clear that she was getting over the shock of an unwanted divorce, wanted privacy. A licking of the wounds, I suppose. We gave her what she wanted—to be left alone. She paid the rent promptly. What else could we want of a tenant? No complaints, no demands."

"But no traffic in lovers?" Quist persisted.

Braden shrugged. "We simply didn't pay any attention.

There weren't any gay parties, that's for sure. Left just ahead, Quist."

"Your wife saw somebody there the night of the murder," Quist said.

"Unlucky for her," Braden said. "Nancy's been forced to look at a thousand faces in a thousand mug books. She says she'd know the man if she saw him again, but I doubt it. I think she could sit next to him at dinner and she wouldn't know him. Just pull up by the front door."

The house was breathtaking, Lydia thought. On one side the fenced-in meadows, the paddocks, the grazing horses. On the other side an expanse of sand dunes with the ocean waves pounding at the beach. There were gardens, and shrubs, and beautifully tended lawns.

"How incredibly lovely!" Lydia said as she got out of the car.

Braden looked up at the great stone house. "My father-in-law built it forty years ago," he said. "A monument to the great god Oil."

Nancy Braden was a surprise. They walked into a great cool entrance hall and she came charging out of some inner room, obviously prepared to launch an attack of some sort. When she saw strangers, she stopped short, her mouth a thin, compressed slit. She was a tall woman, a couple of inches taller than her muscular husband. She was too thin. The aristocratic bone structure of her face, her skin tanned, gave her a gaunt look. Lydia had the notion that Nancy Braden was, somehow, being consumed by tensions.

Braden, smiling, introduced them. "Mr. Quist has an interesting idea, darling, I thought we might discuss over drinks." He turned to his guests. "Nancy and I usually go for martinis at this time of day. But you can name your poison."

"A martini would be fine," Lydia said.

"On the rocks, if possible," Quist said. "With a twist of lemon."

"I'll tell Munson," Nancy Braden said, and took off.

Braden led the way to a comfortable living room with a huge picture window that looked out over the ocean. The sound of the waves was steady, rhythmic.

"Nancy's pretty keyed up by what's happened here," Braden said. "Every time she sees a stranger she thinks it's some new policeman with some new questions."

"She could hardly mistake Lydia for a cop," Quist said.

"The less they look like cops, the more convinced Nancy is that that's what they are," Braden said. He pointed to the oil painting of a beautiful horse on the far wall. "The sire of Golden Belle's dam. He won the Grand National in his day. Riding him over a water jump was like flying a plane." A shadow of sadness passed over Braden's face. "He went down with me in the Gold Cup. It was to have been his last race. Broke his neck. He's buried there, at the place where he fell. A great horse. The greatest over brush and timber I ever rode."

The long gone death of a gallant horse touched him a great deal more deeply than the brutal murder of a woman within a few hundred yards of this room, Lydia thought. Still, he'd gone to the funeral.

Nancy Braden joined them. She had found time to regain at least a social composure. Her smile was brittle, but it was hung out there. She must have been a very handsome girl, Lydia thought; handsome rather than beautiful. She had a kind of awkward style. Horsey.

"We've been saying how lovely your house is, Mrs. Braden," Quist said. "The location, the two contrasting views. Quite sensational."

"My father built it forty years ago," Nancy said. "He gave it to Johnny and me when we were married. There were no stables, or paddocks, or pastures then. My father loved the ocean. Johnny transformed the other part."

Braden explained Quist's "scheme" to his wife. She listened politely, but Lydia had the feeling that she was somewhere else. As Braden talked, an English butler out of *Upstairs, Downstairs* brought drinks and a tray of little cocktail foods. He passed the drinks, the little napkins, the tray of edibles.

"Here's to crime!" Braden said, raising his chilled glass.

"Johnny!" Nancy Braden's protest was sharp.

"Sorry, darling," Braden said. "A stupid cliché." He smiled at his guests. "It's astonishing how, when something unusual happens, things you say take on meanings you hadn't thought of."

"I guess I'm a little edgy," Nancy Braden said. "You can't imagine what it's been like here since—since that night."

"I have a sort of by-product interest in the case, Mrs. Braden," Quist said. "Jim Landis, the woman's ex-husband, works at the Arena. It's bad publicity for us if by any chance he's involved. I wondered about the man you saw and spoke to that night. Could it have been Landis?"

"No," Nancy Braden said positively.

"Your husband says he didn't know him by sight. But you did?"

"To my knowledge I've never seen him," Nancy Braden said. "But the police have shown me pictures of him. He's a big, muscular, athletic-looking man. The man I saw was short, plumpish. Not possibly Landis."

"But it was too dark for you to distinguish his features?"

"Not clearly. But I'm certain I'd know him if I saw him again." Her smile looked pasted on. "I had no reason to pay particular attention to him at the time. I didn't know anything had happened to Allegra. He was just a caller. He said she wasn't at home. I pointed to her car. He said she must have gone off with someone. That was logical. I had no reason at all to imagine he'd killed her."

"And dumped her in the swimming pool."

"It's not a swimming pool," Braden said. "It's just a little lily pond at the back of the cottage. Look, Quist, I understand how fascinating this must be to you, but we've just about had it. Let's talk about jumping contests. Can I refill your glass, Miss Morton?"

Quist and Lydia drove down the winding drive, past the stables, the pastures, the grazing horses, and through the wooded area to the main highway.

"Had you really thought about a jumping contest?" Lydia asked. She was slumped down in the seat beside him, sitting close to him as though she needed the contact.

Quist laughed. "When I saw him schooling that mare. It's not such a bad idea, though. I thought the lady was up awfully tight, didn't you?"

"I might be, too, if somebody had been murdered on my front doorstep," Lydia said. "As a matter of fact, I thought we'd stepped into the middle of some kind of marital war. When we first arrived she came charging out of nowhere, out for his scalp, I thought."

"Maybe." Quist swung wide to pass a farm tractor. "I got the distinct feeling that our Nancy can put the finger on Andrew Crown any time she comes face to face with him. We've spent most of a day without coming any nearer to springing him."

"So what's next?"

"I'd like to ask Jim Landis what extreme mental cruelty was," Quist said. "He got the divorce, remember? I'd like him to convince me he wasn't in bed with his ex-wife the night she was murdered. Damn it, Lydia, I still wish the real Allegra would step forward. Landis will almost certainly give us a different picture than Andrew's."

It was a little after six, the last of the sun disappearing behind the Arena, when they arrived there. Quist was surprised to find the parking area jammed with cars—acres of cars. He maneuvered the Mercedes to an area reserved for employees of the Arena and persuaded the attendant there that he was entitled.

"What are so many cars doing here at this time of day?" Quist asked.

"You might call it a twi-night doubleheader," the man said. "A late afternoon special for elementary school kids. There's twenty thousand screaming little monsters inside. They'll be swarming out here in about twenty minutes. Evening performance at eight."

Drifting out from the Arena came the sound of the circus calliope, and the shrill laughter and applause of children. The attendant pointed to a side entrance which would take Quist directly to Ted Frost's office.

Frost, alone in his office going over what appeared to be box office reports, looked wilted but game. It occurred to Quist that just looking at Lydia tended to revive the young man.

"God, I hate these children's specials!" he said. "The little bastards will steal anything that isn't nailed down. Pictures, signs, even, for God sake, doorknobs! You catch up with Jim Landis?"

"Didn't try," Quist said. "You told us he'd be back for the evening show."

Frost glanced at his wrist watch. "He should be here any minute. Hour and a half before showtime."

"He didn't have to be here for this children's special?"

"Normally, yes. But we gave him time off because of the funeral; told him to skip it. Can I buy you two a drink in the Sponsors' Club? It's soundproofed against the caterwauling of those brats."

The invitation offered a chance to freshen up and they accepted. The Sponsors' Club was reserved for people who had contributed to the original financing of the Arena. Its facilities included a bar as long as a freight train, a gourmet restaurant, plus handball and squash courts, an indoor pool, sauna baths, and a beauty parlor for the ladies. The service was impeccable. There was a sort of glassed-in terrace that looked down into the main arena. You could sit there in a comfortable armchair and watch the show, whatever it might be. Quist found it odd to watch the final circus parade, see the screaming audience of children, and hear nothing. The Club was truly soundproofed.

They had a drink with Frost as the Arena emptied and an army of trash collectors and cleaning people hurried to ready the place for the evening performance. Once the last child had left, Frost took his guests to find Jim Landis. It turned out that Landis was late. A young man who was one of Landis's assistants in the concessions department was surprised because Landis hadn't called in to say he'd be late. It seemed that Landis was almost never late, and on the rare occasions when he had been, he always called in with an explanation and instructions for his staff.

"I got the feeling from something I heard that Landis is a little unpredictable," Quist said to Frost.

Frost shrugged. "As a human being, yes; as a man holding down an important job he's been a hundred percent dependable."

"A health nut, someone told me."

"Body beautiful," Frost said, smiling. "Not health foods and that kind of crap. He's strictly a steak-and-eggs man. But, in his early fifties, he looks as if he could take on Muhammad Ali and give him a hard time. Push-ups, weight lifting, jogging. Women still swoon over him, the lucky jerk!"

"So what's unpredictable about him?" Quist asked.

"He was a pretty wild young man, from all accounts," Frost said. "Reform school, burglary charges, a blackmail charge on which he wasn't convicted, friend of gamblers and confidence people. Scandals over women. And then, twenty-five years ago—he was twenty-eight, twenty-nine—he married Allegra Graves, local girl. Changed man overnight, from all accounts. Raised a family, steady job. He managed a supermarket in the next town. When we needed a man with experience in buying food, dozens of people recommended him. He knew the business and he was great with the public. We were able to offer him a better salary than he was earning, and we felt very lucky to get him. We only opened eighteen months ago, as you know. He'd only been here a few weeks when he divorced his wife. Local people were surprised. Everybody thought it was a perfect marriage. One of the boys was a little wild, the way his old man had been. The other was a good student, solid—more like they thought his mother was."

" 'Thought' his mother was?"

"Well, he got the divorce. No alimony. And her reputation since then."

"That reputation," Lydia said. "True or false?"

"I told you what the talk is," Frost said.

By eight o'clock the Arena was jammed again with customers for the night performance of the circus. Jim Landis hadn't reported for work, nor had there been any word from him.

Quist and Lydia were not in the mood for a circus. Jim Landis, they felt, had the key to what they needed to know about Allegra. Which is the real Allegra?

Since Landis apparently wasn't coming to work, there was only one place they knew to look for him. His home. His new wife might know where he was if he wasn't there. The address Frost gave them took them to a small cottage on the dunes. The windows were brightly lighted as they drove up. As they started up the path the front door was thrown open and a woman's figure was outlined by the light behind her. A warm, throaty voice called out.

"Where have you been, for God sake?" And then, as Quist and Lydia came closer, "I *am* sorry. I thought you were—"

"Your husband, Mrs. Landis? We hoped we'd find him here." Quist introduced himself and Lydia.

Louise Landis—Red to her friends—invited them in. It was obvious that anxiety, not anger, had her uptight.

Quist hadn't spent any time trying to imagine what Jim Landis's "topless tootsie" would be like. Ted Frost's lip-smacking over her suggested something special. Her hair was a bright red-gold color, her own Lydia could have told him. She was wearing a wine-colored housecoat, split down the front so deeply that she might almost as well have been topless. Perhaps this was a little more provocative than nudity would have been, Quist thought. Her bare feet were encased in silver, open-toed sandals, toenails lacquered to the exact color of the housecoat. No jewelry, unless you counted a little wrist watch, diamond-studded. The things that may have been unexpected about Red Landis were her wide gray-green eyes, her generous mouth, her almost ingenuous openness. "One-time call girl" Andrew Crown had suggested. There didn't appear to be anything hard or calculating about this girl.

"I know who you are, Mr. Quist," she said. She gestured toward the far wall of the paneled living room. It was covered with photographs from floor to ceiling. There were photographs of people, of places, of objects. They were obviously the work of a competent photographer who let his camera lens pick up anything that interested him. Off to one side of the collection—not in a place of honor, Quist noticed —was a picture of Quist himself. He had been caught in a conversation with someone not in the picture in the lobby of the Arena.

"Jim is a camera bug, as you probably know," the red-haired girl said. "Never goes anywhere, even on the job, without some kind of camera on him."

54

The room, aside from that wall of photographs, with its picture window looking out toward the ocean, was right out of Grand Rapids. The chairs and the sofa looked comfortable, but selected without any taste for such things. There were no books to be seen, no personalized knickknacks on the tables or the mantel over the red brick fireplace. The fireplace looked as though it had never been used. Off to one side of it was a huge color television set.

"I hate to call people Mister or Miss," Red Landis said. "Can I call you by your first names, since you're friends of Jim's?"

"Of course," Quist said. "I'm Julian."

"And I'm Lydia," Lydia said. "No wonder people call you Red with that marvelous hair."

"I don't want to sail under a false flag, Red," Quist said. "I'm not a friend of Jim's. I've never met him. But I did want to talk to him about something connected with his job. When he didn't show up for work, I hoped we'd find him here."

Red took a cigarette out of a box on the table behind the couch. Her fingers weren't quite steady as she lit it. "It isn't like him," she said. "But this wasn't an ordinary day."

"Oh?" Quist decided to let her tell him.

"You know about his ex? Jim went to her funeral this morning. It was kind of rough for him. But he thought the boys—his two boys—would expect him to go. The oldest one, Patrick, doesn't even know what's happened, unless he saw it on TV or read it in a paper. Jim wasn't able to reach him. David's in the army in Germany. He couldn't get off in time to get here. So Jim thought he should go. Allegra didn't have any family except old Mrs. Potter, who brought her up. I expected he'd be back in the early afternoon. But he didn't show, and he didn't call—which is also unlike him. He always comes when he says he will, or lets me know." She put out her cigarette after only one or two drags on it. "Look, would you two like a drink? I was holding off till Jim came, but I think I need one now. I've got Scotch or gin."

"I think we'll pass," Quist said. "But help yourself."

"I wish you wouldn't," Red said. "I never drink alone. Rule of the house."

"Gin and tonic would be fine," Lydia said. "Can I help you?"

"It's all right there on the sideboard," Red said. "I had it set up for Jim when he came. Jim's a Scotch drinker."

Quist still passed. He waited while ice rattled in glasses and a pouring ceremony took place. The two women sat down on the sofa facing him. Red drank thirstily from her glass.

"It's not like him," she repeated, as though she didn't have the resources to cope with the unexpected.

"Maybe he ran into old friends and tied one on," Quist suggested. "It's happened before this at funerals."

"I don't think so," Red said. She tried lighting another cigarette. "He never drinks before he has to go to work. Oh, maybe a snort before he leaves here—a drink with me. But not drinking, if you know what I mean."

"Did you object to his going to the funeral?" Lydia asked.

"No. Why should I? She no longer mattered to him. He's mine now, you know? He just did what he thought his boys would want him to do. Pay his respects, sort of. I mean, pay *their* respects. Where do you suppose he is?" It was still not anger, but deep concern.

"Did the police bother him after the murder?" Quist asked. Even talking about the crime kept her occupied.

"Oh, sure, they talked to him. I guess everybody who knew her. You see, they don't have any leads—except that guy Mrs. Braden saw and spoke to. Ex-husbands and wives are supposed to be mortal enemies. Husbands don't pay their alimony, and their ex's hate them; wives get tough about it and their ex's hate them. But there wasn't any alimony involved between Jim and Allegra. He got the divorce, you know."

"I'd heard."

"The poor guy was desperate when I met him. She shut the door on him a long time ago, you know."

"The door?"

"The bedroom door. What else? What else drives a guy up the wall?"

Quist gave her a faint smile.

"About a year and a half ago I was working in a joint out on the main drag," Red said. "He came in one night, and I could tell right away he was a gent with troubles. You learn to spot 'em, you know." Talking about him seemed to help her and the words tumbled out. She was talking about a man she loved, Quist thought. "Part of my job was to get the customers to buy drinks; keep 'em talking and buying. If they went too far I could back off—or if I chose I could not back off. I didn't back off with him. He was hurting. The third time we went out together he asked me to marry him." Red glanced at Lydia. "He didn't have to marry me, you understand. He was getting all he asked for. But—that was what he wanted. To marry me. Can you imagine that? He knew what I was. He knew how easy I'd been for him."

"People don't always need time to fall in love," Lydia said.

"I didn't even know what falling in love was—then," Red said. "Anyway, he was already married, but he told me his divorce was in the works."

"Before he met you?"

"Yeah. I had nothing to do with the breakoff between them. So, the divorce came through and we were married that same day." She hesitated a moment, her lips parted. "It was like something I never dreamed of. Oh, I knew how good he was in bed. You never saw him? He's a real hunk of man, friends. But he's kind, and gentle, and thoughtful. I'd walk through fire for him." She crushed out her cigarette. "Today is the first time he's done something I can't account for. I mean, not letting me know where he is, or telling me he wasn't coming home when I expected him. You think—you think there may have been an accident or something?" The question was directed at Lydia.

"When he turns up there'll be a perfectly reasonable explanation," Lydia said. She smiled at Quist. "There always is."

Outside there was the sound of a car stopping, a motor turned off, a door slamming. Red jumped up from the couch and literally ran to the door. She pulled the door open.

"Jim, where—?" Her voice trailed off.

A tall, slender man stood in the doorway. Pale blue eyes behind wire-rimmed glasses looked past Red to Lydia and Quist. The man took a cigarette out of a thin straight mouth.

"Oh, Mr. Bonham!" Red said.

The name rang a bell with Quist. This was the special investigator for the County Prosecutor.

"I'm afraid I have some bad news for you, Mrs. Landis," Bonham said. His voice was cold, emotionless.

Red's hands went up to her mouth. "There's been an accident!" she said.

"Not exactly. May I come in?"

She stood aside. Bonham stepped into the room. "You're Julian Quist, aren't you?" he said. "They told me at the Arena you'd been looking for Landis."

"And haven't found him," Quist said. "This is Miss Morton."

Bonham acknowledged the introduction with a curt nod. "You didn't find him because he's had it," he said.

Lydia stood up and crossed to Red Landis, who still stood by the door, every ounce of color drained from her face.

"Had it?" Quist said.

"The night watchman at St. Peter's Cemetery found him about an hour ago," Bonham said. He glanced at Red. "You might as well have it straight out, Mrs. Landis. He was sprawled over his ex-wife's grave, shot through the head."

"Oh, my God!" It was a strangled whisper from Red.

"Gun in his hand," Bonham said.

"He killed himself?" Quist asked.

"No!" Red cried out. "Never! He'd never do such a thing! He had no reason to do such a thing."

"I'm afraid I must ask you to come with me to the Medical Examiner's office, Mrs. Landis. Official identification."

"Oh, my God," the girl moaned. "I—I'll have to get on some different clothes."

She moved unsteadily, like someone in a trance, toward the back of the house. At a nod from Quist, Lydia followed her. Bonham tossed his cigarette into the fireplace and lit a fresh one.

"No way to duck telling her," he said. His pale eyes fixed on Quist. "I know something about you, Mr. Quist. You've been involved in some criminal cases in the city. We have a mutual friend."

"Who would that be?"

"Lieutenant Kreevich of Manhattan Homicide. Because of that I'm going to tell you how this is. It was meant to look like a suicide."

"Meant to look?"

"Gun in his hand. Shot right between the eyes. But the gun has no serial number; filed off. There are no powder burns around the wound. No powder residue on either of his hands. He couldn't have fired it. He couldn't have shot himself. Somebody murdered him, Mr. Quist, and dumped him there. How long have you been here with the wife?"

PART TWO

CHAPTER ONE

Lieutenant Kreevich of Manhattan Homicide was a slim, wiry man with a boyish face and intense manner. He was a long-time friend of Quist's. He was the new breed of cop: a college education, a law degree. You could spend an evening with Kreevich discussing art, or music, or literature, or politics, but all the time you knew his preoccupation was with law and order. Not the cheap "law and order" of the politicians, but a decent society in which man could live some other way than on the defensive. Kreevich's tastes and Quist's were so alike, their antipathy to violence so strong, that they had become close over the years, sensitive to each other's reactions, trusting each other totally.

While Red Landis was being put through the gruesome business of identifying her husband's body at the Medical Examiner's office, Quist had put in a call to Kreevich in Manhattan.

"About a man named Henry Bonham, who's a special investigator for the County Prosecutor out here on the Island?" Quist asked his friend.

"You two dating each other?" Kreevich asked. "Henry called me about you."

Quist drew his friend a picture of two murders, leaving out Andrew Crown's involvement. "Bonham asked me for help."

It had come about while Red and Lydia had been out of the room at the beach cottage.

"What is your interest in the murder of Allegra Landis?" Bonham had asked. "I happen to know you've been nosing around, Quist."

"If Landis was involved it meant bad publicity for the Arena," Quist said. No mention of Crown, of course. "I didn't want it to explode in our faces without being prepared."

It was hard to tell whether or not Bonham bought it. His pale blue eyes were so cold, almost opaque, behind the gold-rimmed glasses. "I could use some help," he said.

"What kind of help?"

"People loosen up to you who won't to me—or any cop," Bonham had said. "I know you've talked to Eliot Keyes, the Bradens, and Mrs. Landis." A nod toward the bedroom where Lydia was helping Red.

"You've been having me tailed?"

"Small town, large gossip."

"What do you want me to do?"

"Listen. Tell me what you hear."

"If I hear anything worthwhile," Quist had said, evading a direct answer.

Now Kreevich gave Bonham a plus rating. "Henry's a good man," Kreevich said. "I told him you're a good man. Now you can get married. Seriously, Julian, Henry's a first-class investigator and a square shooter. You can help him safely, if your conscience will let you."

"What's my conscience got to do with it?"

"Handling bad publicity for the Arena is a job for your third assistant office boy," Kreevich said. "Maybe, sometimes, you'll tell me what your real interest is."

You didn't slide anything past Kreevich. He was quite right, of course. Quist wouldn't be out here on the Island, snooping around, just to shut off gossip about an Arena employee. There was a competent publicity staff at the Arena and people in the New York office of Julian Quist Associates to handle that kind of thing. Ten to one Kreevich was already thinking Andrew Crown, because he knew that Quist was about to involve himself in Crown's political campaign. If Bonham also knew that he, too, could be thinking.

Quist wondered how far he could go with Bonham? How far should he go? To tell him what he knew about Andrew's night at Allegra's cottage would blow the political campaign. Andrew would be exposed as the man Nancy Braden had seen. She would identify him. Bonham would have to put Andrew on the grill. The agitated man Nancy Braden had seen was in all the news and broadcast accounts. If it was revealed that he was Andrew Crown, candidate for the United States Senate, the ball game would be over. Even if they came up with a murderer there would be questions. What was Andrew's connection with Allegra? What was he doing there? Would anyone doubt that he'd been having an affair with Allegra? Voters were not likely to be charmed by a man who is having affairs behind the back of his crippled wife. Andrew's one chance was to be kept out of this entirely.

So, as Andrew Crown's friend and ally, he couldn't play it all out with Bonham. He couldn't reveal the fact that Andrew had been at the cottage the night of the murder. He couldn't tell Bonham there had been a lover with whom Allegra had been enjoying herself. If Bonham knew this, his own directions would change and the spotlight would focus on Andrew. Quist had accepted Andrew's story was truth; Bonham might not. Damn Kreevich for mentioning his conscience! It was already bothering him.

Quist realized that he had allowed himself to be convinced that the real Allegra Landis was Andrew Crown's version.

She had not been ready for Andrew or anyone else. She had turned Andrew down on that account. If true, then it appeared to be dead certain that the lover Andrew had heard in her bed was her ex-husband, the man she had loved for twenty-five years. She would take Jim Landis back if that's how it was. But who would kill her for that? Almost certainly Bonham would be attracted to Andrew, the rejected would-be lover. He heard what was going on, he came back later, he punished her. That would be logical reasoning for Bonham if he knew what Quist knew. Following that line, Bonham would ask himself another question. Where was Andrew Crown when Jim Landis was shot and draped over Allegra's grave? Surely it would seem likely that the same person had punished both lovers. What else could Bonham think?

Andrew had better damn well have a rock-ribbed alibi for his day, from the time of the funeral and on through the rest of the day and evening.

Lydia had stayed with Red Landis through the gruesome business of identification. Quist, waiting in an anteroom outside the Medical Examiner's office, thought it was taking a hell of a long time. Bonham, in all probability, was asking questions. He had asked Quist a question that indicated his early thinking. How long, he had wanted to know, had Quist and Lydia been with Red at the dune cottage? Clichés are more often accurate than not. A violently dead husband suggests a violently angry wife.

Quist lit one of his long, thin cigars and began to pace the anteroom restlessly. He didn't buy the angry wife. Red's anxiety, her obvious love for her missing husband, had, Quist was convinced, been genuine. Red couldn't have fooled both him and Lydia. Yet Bonham would have to toy with the idea of a jealous wife killing both lovers.

To get Andrew Crown and Red Landis off the hook, Quist knew he had to come at the problem from a different tangent.

66

The real Allegra was not Andrew's Allegra. The real Allegra was Ted Frost's concept, the sexy divorcée ready to take on the whole town. The real Allegra had played Andrew for a sucker, six hundred dollars' worth of sucker. She hadn't had time for a conscience-burdened older man with all the young available studs in Cranville. The lover Andrew had heard in her bed had not been Jim Landis. It could have been any one of a dozen eager beavers. And murder? She had played Andrew for a few hundred dollars; maybe, having granted more generous favors, she had played someone else for a great deal more. Was the real Allegra not only a sexpot but a blackmailer?

But why would a blackmailed murderer go after Jim Landis?

If the real Allegra was Andrew's Allegra, why would she have "shut the door on Jim," as Red had said, and then have taken him back so readily for a night of love?

The door to the anteroom burst open and a young man charged in. He was tall, slim, wearing blue jeans and a leather jacket over a plaid sports shirt. He had a dark beard and hair worn very long.

"Where are they?" he demanded of Quist.

"Where are who?"

"My mother and father!" the young man almost shouted.

"Who are you?"

"Patrick Landis," the young man said. "They said I'd find my father and mother here."

Quist hesitated. Did you tell this young man with wild dark eyes that his mother was buried and his father was in an icebox in the next room?

It had happened to Quist before—a sudden revulsion to violence that urged him to drop his involvement and get away from it. Looking at Patrick Landis, he decided the only thing in the world he wanted was to get Lydia away from here, take her back to their apartment on Beekman Place in the city, and forget about Allegra and Jim Landis, forget about Andrew Crown and Red Landis, and involve himself with the only things that really mattered—his woman, his work.

Sometimes Quist told himself that he must have some sort of internal magnet that attracted violence. He had come face to face with it time and time again over the years. "Typhoid Julian," he had called himself to Lydia once; wherever he went he carried the virus of violence with him. Lydia, quite rational, had pointed out to him that his work took him to where violence was inevitable—a world of glamorous personalities, big money, desperate competition. Violence in this world, exposed, became a part of everyone's world, everyone's TV fare, spotlighted, headlined.

"But there is just as much violence in climates that aren't so interesting to the general public," Lydia had said. "People turn violent because they've lost in some struggle for survival, lost a woman, lost a man, burned themselves up with jealousy, with hate, with greed. You don't carry a virus, love. One of the things that's rare about you is that you are immune to the infection that turns men into monsters."

She had been lying beside him in his bed when she'd said that, and he had taken her in his arms, held her close, and murmured that, without her, he could easily become the monster to end all monsters. Serious talk turned to love talk. The two of them together turned into one enormously satisfying whole.

Looking at Patrick Landis, Quist fought the urge to just turn his back and walk out. To hell with Allegra and who she really was; to hell with Jim Landis and Red Landis and this boy. He couldn't do anything for any of them. He didn't need the enormous fee the supporters of Andrew Crown would pay him for handling a campaign. He didn't need the money. He didn't, for God sake, need the problem.

But he stood looking at the young man with the wild, red-rimmed eyes. Red-rimmed from the sun? From swimming in the salt ocean? From tears? He must be about twenty-four, Quist thought, born in the first year of Allegra's marriage to Jim Landis. A love child, a wanted child, in some kind of big trouble, Andrew had said. Allegra had tried to raise money for him.

"My name is Quist," Quist said. "I am one of your father's employers. How much do you know about what's happened?"

"Not very damned much!" Patrick's voice was harsh. "On, for God sake, a car radio. I was hitchhiking. My father committed suicide, the radio said. And then—then they reminded the listeners that Allegra had been butchered a few days ago and that my father shot himself on her grave." He turned his face away. "Oh, God!"

"You hadn't known about your mother?"

"I've been thumbing my way here from Arizona," Patrick said. "I guess no one in Missouri or Ohio or Pennsylvania gave a damn what happened to Allegra."

He called his mother by her first name, but he referred to Jim Landis as "my father."

"How did it happen?" Patrick asked. "I mean, to Allegra."

"You may not have the stomach for it," Quist said. "She was stabbed to death and her nude body thrown in the pool back of her cottage. Do you know the place?"

Patrick looked dazed. "No. No—I never saw the cottage. Allegra didn't find it until I'd been gone quite a while. Do they know who—?"

"Not yet," Quist said.

The boy's mouth took an anguished downward twist, like the classic mask of Tragedy. "Poor Allegra. She never harmed anyone. She was never anything but kind to anyone. Why? Why, *why?*" His eyes glittered. "When they find the sonofabitch, I swear to God I'll—"

The door at the end of the room opened and Lydia came through it with Red Landis leaning heavily on her arm for support. It was instantly obvious, from the exchange of blank looks, that Patrick had no idea who Red was, nor she who he was.

"Red, this is Pat Landis," Quist said.

"Oh, my God!" she whispered.

"Your father's widow," Quist said to Pat.

The young man's face was dark with anger again. "My father's whore, you mean!"

Red turned her tear-stained face away as though this was the climax of an unendurable time. Lydia gave Pat Landis a look that should have withered him. "There are jerks, and there are jerks," she said. "Go to the head of the class." And she hustled Red out of the room and toward the parking lot.

Quist left Patrick standing there alone and followed them out. Lydia was rarely angry, but she was steaming now.

"They ask her a dozen insinuating questions after they show her a body without a face, and then they turn her loose to handle things by herself. Then that little bastard!" She turned to Red, almost crooning. "Come on, love, into the car. We'll go somewhere and get blind together."

Red was planted in the front seat to sit between them. Quist, behind the wheel, could feel the girl's body shaking like someone with a malarial chill.

"I wanted to say it wasn't him," she said in a choked voice. "It couldn't be him—with no face. Yet I knew it was him— the way the hair grew on the backs of his hands, the little mole on his chest, intimate things. Oh, God!" She turned to Lydia. "You'd know Julian, wouldn't you, if they took away his face?"

"I'd know him," Lydia said.

"Mr. Bonham talked as though he thought I might have killed Jim," Red said. "As if he didn't think it was suicide!"

She sounded bewildered.

"He's convinced it wasn't suicide," Quist said. "No powder marks around the wound. When you fire a handgun it leaves powder marks in the palm of your hand. There were none. Tell me, Red, did Jim own a gun?"

She simply didn't get it. "Mr. Bonham asked me that. I never saw a gun. If he had one at work he never mentioned it to me. He—he was working on some kind of security system at the Arena, but I don't know if that included his having a gun there."

"What kind of security system?"

"I don't know, Julian. Something about cameras—but I don't know!"

"Can't we let it drop for now?" Lydia asked. She was still angry. She was holding Red's hand firmly in hers. "You don't have to go back to your house if you don't want to, Red. You can come into the city with us, stay with us if you like."

"I—I think I'd like to go home," Red said, her voice unsteady. "In a way—in a way, Jim is still there." She lifted brimming eyes to Lydia. "Can you—understand that, Lydia?"

"Of course. Is there someone who would stay with you?"

Red shook her head. "There's no one that close. I mean —Jim is—was—my whole life."

"I'll stay with you if you like," Lydia said.

"Oh, would you? Could you? I mean, just for tonight, Lydia. Just till it's daylight again."

"Of course," Lydia said. She looked over the top of the girl's lowered head at Quist, as if daring him to debate the matter.

The dune cottage was just as they had left it, lights burning in the living room and the bedrooms. Red Landis muttered something about "putting on a new face," waved vaguely at the bar, and left Quist and Lydia.

"I couldn't let her stay alone, if she needed someone," Lydia said.

"You're a good person," Quist said. He needed to touch her, and he moved close to her and held her in his arms, his lips brushing the dark hair above her forehead. "It doesn't any of it make much sense," he said after a moment. "Whatever her past, Red seems to be a pretty decent, uncomplicated human being. Is she too simpleminded and without normal intuitions not to have guessed that her man was having an affair with his ex-wife?"

"I don't think he was," Lydia said. "I've changed my mind about him, Julian. I think his alibi may be good."

"So explain why someone would kill him and try to make it look as if he'd shot himself, grieving over Allegra's death?"

"Someone who didn't know too much about guns and the traces they leave," Lydia said.

Quist bent down and kissed his woman's lips. Then he turned away from her, toward the telephone on a corner table. "I want to make sure Andrew has been where he's supposed to have been all day," he said. "I don't know why, but I have an uneasy feeling about him."

The Crowns lived in Cove Town, about ten miles from Cranville. Quist found their phone number in the book and dialed. A sharp, edgy woman's voice answered after the first ring.

"Mrs. Crown?"

"Yes."

"Marjorie, this is Julian Quist. I'm sorry to call at this time of night." Quist's watch told him that it was almost one in the morning. "But it's important that I talk to Andrew."

"He's not here," Marjorie Crown said. "I thought this call might be from him."

"Where is he?"

The woman's voice was bitter. "I haven't the faintest idea, Julian."

For the second time that night a woman was waiting for the answer to an unexplained absence of her man. Quist could visualize her, sitting in her wheelchair, a robe draped over her useless legs, waiting next to the telephone which hadn't rung until now.

"Didn't he tell you where he was going, Marjorie?"

"He doesn't have to account to me!"

"When did he leave you?"

"Hours, days, months ago, depending on what you mean by the question, Julian."

"Fact," Quist said sharply. "When did he go out?"

"This morning—yesterday morning—whatever. About ten o'clock, to be exact. He said he'd be back in a little while. He wasn't."

"And he hasn't called you?"

"No."

"Is that usual?"

"No. Oh, it's usual for him to be away. But normally he comes back when he says he will—or lets me know. Normally I can depend on that."

"Look, Marjorie, it's very important that I talk to him whenever he does come back. I'm in Cranville. Would it upset you if I came over there to wait for him?"

There was a curious break in her voice as she answered. "I'd be grateful, Julian."

Marjorie Crown had been a very beautiful woman not too long ago. Quist remembered her, dark, athletic, an amateur golf champion, a magnificent swimmer. She'd had an electric vitality. She was, he guessed, about forty now, fifteen years younger than her husband. She had oozed confidence in herself, her marriage, her life. There had been no children, reason unknown.Perhaps by choice. Andrew's and Marjorie's togetherness, to use a corny phrase, was so total they may not have wanted anything to interfere with it.

And then a dark night, with fog sweeping in off the ocean. Marjorie, who drove a car with the skill of a professional race driver, approaching a crossing that had no stop sign or lights, arrives at the same instant that a giant trailer truck plunges out of the mist. Her skills, her quick reflexes, were not good enough for the crisis. In one grinding, ripping moment Marjorie Crown was transformed from a vital, alive, exciting woman into an embittered cripple, paralyzed from the waist down. Quist hadn't seen her since the accident. She saw no one, Andrew had told him, except one or two older women friends. She'd had a special excitement for men before the accident, flirted expertly, remained elusive to everyone but Andrew. Now that was gone, she knew. She couldn't bear to have men look at her with pity in their eyes. Rumor had it that she had taken to drinking too much, but who could blame her? What else was there?

And Quist knew that Andrew had, in his own despair, been attracted elsewhere; by Allegra. But which Allegra?

The Crowns' house, a Spanish-style stucco villa, looked down on the cove that gave Cove Town its name. It was a mile or so out of the village, away from any street lights or electric signs, and it stood out against the night sky like a jewel, lights blazing in every window. There must be someone in the house beside Marjorie, Quist thought—someone who took care of her.

Quist left his car and walked up the path to the front door, heavy oak with wrought-iron hinges. It opened before he could reach the knocker. Just inside Marjorie Crown sat in her wheelchair, eyes bright, angry, defensive. Let him show one vestige of pity and she would rip him to pieces, Quist thought.

"Hello, Marjorie," he said quietly. "Long time no see."

The wheelchair worked with electric controls. She swung it away to let him in. She even handled a wheelchair with style, he thought. As he stepped into the brightly lighted entrance hall, he got a good look at her once lovely face. There were new lines in it, etched there by pain and, probably, self-pity. The once wide, laughing, generous mouth was a straight, compressed slit.

Without a word she led the way into a small sitting room, obviously set up specially for her. There was a space into which she neatly maneuvered the chair. She was surrounded on her right by a well-stocked little bar, behind her a writing desk with a portable typewriter on it which she could reach by swinging the chair around in a full turn, and at her left a circular bookcase that could be revolved to present her with what she wanted. In front of her was a shelf that swung on hinges from the bar, on which she could place a drink, a book, an ash tray. There was a tray there now, just about overflowing with cigarette butts.

Quist had not remembered her extraordinary eyes, hazel in color. They looked oddly bright as she stared at him, as though she was suffering from a fever, or—he thought reluctantly—there were drugs involved. They might be used to deal with the pain. He didn't know whether there was physical pain. God knows there was plenty of pain of another kind.

"Before we dissolve into polite chitchat, Julian," she said in a dead-level voice, "I'd like to ask you a direct question, and I'd like a direct answer. No attempt to protect my feelings, as if I had any."

"Shoot," Quist said.

"Do you know something I don't know about Andrew? Are you here to soften some kind of a blow?"

"I just know that I need to talk to him," Quist said. "We launch the campaign on Monday. Things pop up that need his advice and consent."

"At one-thirty in the morning?"

"I'm sorry, Marjorie. I didn't dream I'd get you on the phone when I called. Andrew knows that there aren't any specific office hours when you're planning to fire your big guns."

She pulled the little shelf toward her, took a cigarette from an open pack and put it between her lips. The hand that held her monogrammed lighter wasn't steady. "You are a lousy liar, Julian," she said. She flicked a nonexistent ash into the overflowing tray.

Quist took a step toward her. "Can I empty that for you?" He reached for the tray.

She snatched the tray away, spilling some of its contents on the shelf. "I don't need your pity, Julian!" she cried out in a shrill voice. "I'm quite competent to take care of my own needs."

He drew a deep breath and his face hardened. "While you sit there wallowing in self-pity," he said, "have you forgotten there are little courtesies that some men still offer to women, like standing when they come into the room, like letting them go through a door first, like holding a chair to seat them at the dinner table, like emptying their ash trays? I wasn't feeling pity for you, Marjorie. It was just a normal reflex. You act more like a snapping turtle than a woman, which doesn't move me to feel pity of any sort."

She stared at him as though he had unexpectedly slapped her. Then she lowered her face and covered it with shaking hands.

"Oh God, oh God, oh God!" she whispered.

Quist picked up the ash tray and dumped its overflow into a basket by the bar. "May I make myself a drink?" he asked in a conversational tone.

She gave him a go-ahead gesture, unable to speak. He poured himself a stiff slug of bourbon on the rocks. She had guessed right, of course. He had lied to her, but not in the way she imagined. She thought he was holding back the news of some sort of accident. She couldn't guess, he was sure, that he was hiding her husband's interest in another woman, his possible involvement in a murder. Nor could he tell her any of this without Andrew's consent. Where the hell was Andrew?

He pulled up a Windsor chair and sat down facing the woman who was still fighting for control. He had played it tough with her, and he couldn't guess what the end result would be. After a long time she looked up at him. She actually smiled at him. It was the ghost of a gay smile he remembered.

"In the words of the immortal television commercial," she said. " 'Thanks, I needed that.' "

He had made the right move.

"If only Andrew would play it tough with me instead of being so damned concerned, so gentle," she said.

"Let's face it," Quist said. "I feel sorry for you. Wouldn't you feel sorry for me if I lost an arm or a leg? But you wouldn't admire me if I turned my back on life, Marjorie. Andrew needs you as an active force in his life. I need you, for God sake, as his campaign manager. I need you active in that campaign, showing the world what a gutsy person you really are."

"Oh, Julian!"

"You've turned that wheelchair into a premature coffin!"

She put out her cigarette in the tray, her eyes wide and fixed on him. "Do you really think I could help?"

"Of course you could help. First of all by giving him back some joy in his marriage. He loves you. Turn it back into a going concern and not into a perpetual wake."

"Joy!" The bitterness crept back into her voice.

"Sex isn't everything," Quist said. "And if you'd stop grieving over yourself you might even find some ways for reviving that. But companionship, partnership, mutual interests." He shrugged. "Duck soup."

"You don't know what it was like—before that night," she said. "It was so complete, so total. 'Joy' is the right word for what it was."

"I do know what it was like," Quist said. "I'm lucky enough to have a woman who gives me what you gave to Andrew before you started to mourn for yourself."

"Lydia?"

"Who else?"

"How is she?"

"She's fine. She sent her love by the way."

"Would you mind making me a gin and tonic, Julian?"

Victory, he thought. She was letting herself be helped. He got up, went to the bar, and made her drink for her. When he handed it to her she held it up to the light for a moment, swirling the liquid around the ice cubes. She smiled at him. It was a slightly more vigorous ghost of the past.

"Has someone told you that I've become an alcoholic, Julian? Because this is a drink you might have made for your maiden aunt from Peoria. Just a little more gin, please."

He added an ounce and brought it back to her.

"It's been so difficult, Julian," she said after she'd sipped the drink and nodded approval. "In the space of a few hours I stopped being anything I'd ever been to Andrew. I was out of his bed forever. I couldn't share in his recreation. We used to play golf together, go to the theater, dances at the country club, pleasant parties. I couldn't be his hostess at those parties."

"You thought."

"In some ways I was a vain woman. I was proud of my looks, proud of my body, proud of my social graces, my wit, my charm. I would have been better off dead than the way I was. But God help me, Julian, I was afraid to die."

"You can still be proud of all those things, plus your courage if you show any," Quist said.

"Damn you, Julian!" But she was smiling. Then the clouds

returned. "You can't shut off a man's pleasures just because you can't provide them any longer. I told him to find himself a woman who would substitute for me in bed. And I knew I would hate him if he did. After a while there came a stretch of time—quite recently—when he began to work late at the office, stopped coming home for dinner two or three nights a week. I was sure he had found someone. He assured me he hadn't, but I didn't believe him. Would you believe I used to go through his clothes looking for something, I don't know what, that would prove I was right. I would actually sniff at his shirts to see if I could detect an unfamiliar perfume. When he decided on this political thing I was pleased for him, and at the same time I was certain if he got out in the world he'd find someone else. I've given him a very bad time." She took a long swallow of her drink. "Tell me the truth, Julian. I can take it. Is there another woman?"

There had been Allegra, of course, but not in quite the way Marjorie imagined. Allegra hadn't been ready for Andrew or anyone else—she'd said. Perhaps Andrew's unsatisfied hunger was worse than if he'd had it.

"There's no woman on earth he cares for," Quist said. A miserable truth.

She looked as if he'd lifted the world off her shoulders. "And you really think I could help in the campaign if I—"

"If you went to the beauty parlor—"

"Do I look such a horror, Julian?"

"It's how you feel you look that matters. If you get out into the world, get positive, get alive—"

"Julian!" She raised a hand for silence.

From outside he heard the sound of a car. Then the motor died and there was the sound of a garage door being pulled shut. Quist glanced at his watch. A quarter past two.

A key turned in the front door lock and Andrew came in, looking haggard and, Quist thought, a little drunk. Quist's car had told Andrew that there was someone unexpected in the house. When he saw Quist, he looked relieved.

"I thought—there was some kind of trouble," he said.

Marjorie held out her hands to her husband, and the smile was no longer forced. "Darling, I was beginning to be worried about you. But I've had a lovely time with Julian."

Andrew looked bewildered. He went over to her and she reached up and pulled his face down to hers. She kissed him.

"And now I'm off to bed," Marjorie said. "Julian has campaign problems to discuss with you, darling."

"Sleep well," Andrew said in a dull voice.

"I'll be up early to make an appointment with the hairdresser," Marjorie said.

"You—you're going out?"

"Don't worry. Mrs. Coggins will drive me. Good night, you two."

The wheelchair made a buzzing sound as she guided it swiftly out of the room.

"What on earth have you done to her?" Andrew asked when they heard her bedroom door close.

"I think," Quist said, "I've persuaded her to get off her butt and start living. Now, friend, will you please tell me where you've been and what you've been up to?"

Andrew Crown had been "nowhere in particular" for sixteen hours, since yesterday morning at ten.

"I decided I had to go to Allegra's funeral," he said.

"You idiot."

Quist had followed Andrew into his study, a soundproofed room. It was safe to talk there.

"I know," Andrew said. He had dropped down in the chair behind his desk. He looked gray with fatigue. "I—I wasn't right there, you understand. I was on a higher piece of ground in the cemetery, watching from a distance."

"Didn't it occur to you the Bradens might be there? That she'd spot you and the game would be over before it started?"

"She wasn't there," Andrew said. "He was there, but she wasn't."

"Lucky you."

"Damn it, Julian, I think I loved Allegra. I simply couldn't not be there to—to see her off!"

"What sentimental crap!" Quist said. "I told you to stay put here until we got some kind of a lead. You may just have put your head very squarely on the block. You know about Landis?"

Andrew nodded his head very slowly, as if it was almost too heavy to move.

"How did you know?"

"Car radio."

"When?"

"A couple of hours ago, I guess." Andrew lifted heavy lids. "That really closes it out, doesn't it, Julian? He killed her and then—then shot himself today. Guilt. Remorse."

"He didn't shoot himself," Quist said. "He was murdered. And the killer draped him over Allegra's grave."

Andrew sat bolt upright in his chair. "But they said it was suicide on the radio!"

"They thought at first it was. It was made to look that way. But no powder burns around the wound or on his hands. He couldn't have shot himself or fired the gun."

"But why—?"

"Bonham is letting the original story stand for the moment. He's letting the killer feel safe as long as he can."

"Bonham is the special investigator?"

"And a very bright, shrewd cop, if you care. Let Nancy Braden identify you and his next question is going to be where you were today. Landis was at the funeral. You were at the funeral. What then? Where have you been for the last fourteen to sixteen hours?"

Andrew leaned back in his chair, pressing his fingertips against his closed eyelids.

"Who do you think she was making love with that night you were there, Andrew? If she was the woman you've described to me, it could only have been one person: the man she'd been in love with most of her adult life. Her ex-husband."

"If that's so, why did he kill her?" Andrew asked. "He had an alibi, they said."

"He was supposed to be at the Arena," Quist said. "He wasn't missed so the Arena people assume he was there. But that doesn't mean he was there."

"So why did he kill her?" Andrew repeated.

"You dumb ape, don't you see how it will read if Bonham comes across your trail? You went there, you discovered her making love to Landis, you waited till he was gone and then you killed her. Outraged would-be lover. She'd betrayed you. Then you waited for an opportune moment and killed him. Both people punished."

"Oh, Jesus!" Andrew said.

"So you better snap out of it, buster, and tell me where you've been since yesterday morning at the funeral," Quist said.

"You don't believe any of that, do you, Julian?"

"It doesn't matter what I believe. What matters is what I can prove—if I have to."

Andrew sat very still, seeming to have shrunk a little inside his clothes. "Would you believe I don't really know?" Andrew said in a small voice.

"Oh, come on, Andrew!"

"Incidentally, Landis wasn't at the funeral."

"What are you talking about? He took time off from his job to be there."

"I don't care. He wasn't there."

"You knew him by sight?"

"Yes." Andrew moistened his lips. "I was curious about him because of Allegra. I made a point of seeing him several times. I even had a drink and some conversation with him one night in the bar at the Arena. I wanted to know the kind of man she had loved."

"Did he know about your interest in Allegra?"

"No. Of course he didn't. We talked about sports. He had a camera with him. Photography was his hobby. He showed me some candid shots he'd taken of some famous people who'd been at the Arena. So, you see, I couldn't have missed him if he'd been at the funeral. It isn't as though there'd been a crowd there. There was almost no one."

"So let's get back to where you've been since the funeral."

"I told you," Andrew said wearily, "I don't really know. I—I just drove around. Out almost to the end of the Island, I think."

"And you just drove for fifteen hours?"

"I stopped for gas someplace."

"Where?"

"I don't know."

"You pay for it with a credit card or cash?"

"Cash."

"You stopped somewhere for a drink. You smell like a saloon."

"I had a flask in the car."

"Food?"

"No."

"And you just drove and drove?"

"Not exactly, Julian. There was a place somewhere— maybe fifty miles from here—where there was a sort of viewpoint; place where you could pull your car off the road and sit and look at the ocean. I stopped there toward the end of the afternoon."

"Anyone see you?"

"I don't know. God, Julian, I didn't care if anyone saw me or not. I wasn't hiding from anything or anyone."

"So you sat looking at the ocean."

"I was pretty exhausted," Andrew said. "I—I haven't slept for days. Emotionally exhausted. So I fell asleep and I must have slept for hours. It was nearly midnight when I woke up. I was cold, and I drank a little from my flask. Then —then I headed for home. That's all there is."

"And no one checked on you? No state trooper patrolling the roads stopped to see if you were alive or dead?"

"I guess not."

"I'd hate to hear you tell that story to the cops if you start to smell gamey to them," Quist said.

"I wasn't trying to supply myself with an alibi, Julian."

Quist's face looked tense in the shadows. "Did you ever write any letters to Allegra?"

"I'm afraid I did. Pretty impassioned love letters. You'd probably think they were schoolboyish."

"I might think they could hang you," Quist said. "Did Allegra keep those letters?"

"I don't know. Probably not. You see, she wasn't in love with me."

"If she kept them you're in big trouble," Quist said. "I'm hoping she didn't. If she had, I think Bonham would have been here long before this."

"I—I don't think so," Andrew said. "You see—well, Marjorie was convinced I was having all sorts of affairs. So I didn't use my stationery, in case a letter got returned for some reason. I wasn't sure Marjorie wouldn't open my mail. I typed the letters on a plain sheet of paper in my office. I didn't sign them. I just wrote the letter Y at the bottom."

" 'Y'?"

"Yours," Andrew said. "Unless she told someone about the letters and who they were from—if she kept them—" Andrew hesitated. "What's the next move, Julian?"

"I wish to God I knew," Quist said.

CHAPTER TWO

And so there were three days left before Andrew Crown's campaign for a seat in the United States Senate was to be launched, or abandoned. The last thing Andrew said to Quist in the early hours of the morning of the second day was that he would not embark on the campaign, begin spending the money his friends and supporters had contributed, if there was danger the whole thing would blow up in their faces. If the police hadn't come up with answers before Monday, Andrew would back off.

"You'll have to explain the why of it to Marjorie," Quist said.

"God help me—and her, but if I have to I have to," Andrew said. He looked wistfully at Quist. "Do you really think you've managed to make a change in her, Julian?"

"I think she loves you, which is no change. I think she's prepared to stop feeling sorry for herself, which is a big change."

"Don't give up on me, Julian. Not just yet."

Quist agreed not to give up, but he didn't tell Andrew that he was not hopeful. He was forced to operate with one hand tied behind his back. He couldn't cooperate with Bonham without revealing Andrew's involvement. He couldn't expect help from Bonham without telling the detective what his real interest in the murders was.

He made two phone calls from Andrew's study at three o'clock in the morning. One was to Lydia at Red Landis's dune cottage. He was going back into the city. He needed help he could only get there. Did she want to go back in with him?

"I can't leave Red," Lydia said. "She's in very bad shape, Julian. When will you be coming back out here?"

"I can't say yet, love. It depends. I'll call you."

"If you have a chance and could bring me some fresh clothes—"

"Do my best. I love you, you know. Why don't we take off for the other side of the world and forget all these creeps?"

"They are people in trouble, Julian. You wouldn't go if I said yes. That's why I love you."

The second call was to Lieutenant Mark Kreevich, who sounded irritated at being waked at that hour, but who quickly agreed to be ready for Quist when he got there—in an hour and a half.

Kreevich was prepared for a guest when Quist rang the doorbell of his apartment at a quarter to five in the morning. The pale light of dawn was beginning to show behind Manhattan's skyline. Kreevich had made coffee and there was a bottle of Jack Daniel's and two glasses on his living-room table.

Quist sat down at the table and drank a slug of whiskey neat.

"You look beat," Kreevich said. He himself looked fresh, shaven, wearing a pair of gray slacks and a navy blue sports shirt. He was ready for whatever. He was a friend.

"I've been on the go since early yesterday morning," Quist said.

"You've got some kind of a mess out there. You ready to tell me what it's all about?"

"Provided you consider what I tell you privileged."

Kreevich's eyes narrowed against the smoke from his cigarette. "Provided you're not reporting a crime in my jurisdiction," he said.

And so Quist told his friend the whole story, Andrew's

story. He told him everything that had happened since then, who he had seen and talked with, Andrew's vulnerability and his lack of alibis for either murder.

They said of Kreevich in the department that he never took notes during an inquiry. His mind was like a computer, they said. Feed it facts and they stayed there, ready for total recall when they were needed. He listened to Quist, lighting fresh cigarettes from the stubs of the ones that had preceded them. He never interrupted with a question. He never spoke until Quist reached for a second slug of Jack Daniel's, indicating that he was finished.

"Bonham could undoubtedly fill in a lot of blank spaces if you chose to confide in him," Kreevich said.

"I can't, and you must see why I can't. My concern is for Andrew Crown. If I drag him into it he's had it. Solving murders isn't my job, Mark. Except that solving them would leave Andrew in the clear."

"Solving them isn't easy for either you or Bonham unless you pool your knowledge," Kreevich said. He poured coffee for himself. "You make it clear that Bonham would instantly suspect Crown if he knew your facts. Have you stopped to do a little suspecting of Crown on your own?"

"Andrew a killer?" Quist laughed.

"Late loves do strange things to people," Kreevich said. "There is a desperateness about last chances. To get turned down in your twenties only seems like a disaster. To get turned down in your late fifties, early sixties, is a disaster. No second chances. No starting over. Something could explode inside a man who has always been kind and gentle. Don't overlook the accident to Crown's wife. That could have thrown his operating mechanism completely out of balance. Under stress he doesn't react the way you might expect him to. He kills the woman who castrated him. Because that's what a rejection is at that time of life—a castration. And he kills the man he thinks was her collaborator." Kreevich grinned at Quist. "End of speech," he said.

Quist wasn't laughing any more. "Give that argument to Bonham and Andrew is on his way to a murder-one indictment," he said. "But—I don't think so, Mark. My whole life, my work, like yours, involves listening to people, sifting the truth from lies and half-truths. I wouldn't be as good as I am if I didn't have an instinct for it. I think Andrew is telling me the truth. I don't think he killed anyone or even thought of killing anyone. When he came to me he was putting it on the line."

"So you have to follow your instinct."

"Let me make one thing clear," Quist said. "I think he's told me the truth as he knows it. That doesn't mean Allegra Landis was the woman he thought she was. Andrew would like to think that she was making love to Landis the night of her murder because he could accept that with less pain than anything else. But that doesn't mean she was with her husband."

"How well off, financially, is Crown?" Kreevich asked.

"Well off."

"He loaned her six hundred dollars?"

"Not important money to him," Quist said.

"So she turns him off. Not ready for him, not for anyone. An affair with him, she says, has the wrong chemistry for her at this time. But, after he'd anguished enough, she might reconsider—and hit him for a really meaningful amount."

"The first amount was for the boy, Patrick, who turned up on the Island tonight. He hitchhiked his way from Arizona. Maybe he needs more money."

"Maybe Allegra was working to get it for him," Kreevich said. "By maneuvering Crown, by crawling into the hay with someone else."

"So she never was the Allegra Crown saw," Quist said.

"I'd assume that if I were investigating the case," Kreevich said.

"So where do I go from here, Mark?"

Kreevich took a deep drag on his cigarette and exhaled the smoke in a long, slow sigh. "You need Bonham's help," he said. "Maybe you can get it by helping him."

"My hands are tied."

"Not all ways," Kreevich said. "Crown told you something that Bonham may not know. He told you Jim Landis wasn't at the funeral. Landis gave the funeral as an excuse for taking time off to his boss at the Arena. You took his presence there for granted. Probably Bonham has, too. It seems important to find out where Landis really was."

"I can't tell Bonham how I know Landis wasn't there."

"But you can verify it another way and tell him," Kreevich said. "Didn't Rooster Braden tell you Landis wasn't there?"

Quist tried to remember exactly. "He didn't tell me he wasn't there. He said there were only ghouls, newspaper people, an old lady who brought her up, and—and himself. He didn't say Landis wasn't there, but he didn't say he was."

"The old lady who brought her up would know. Bonham probably never asked her or Braden. He took Landis's presence for granted, just as you did. Ask the old lady and you may have something to give to Bonham without involving Crown. Your interest in Landis is legitimate and you've established it with Bonham."

"Of course you're right," Quist said. "Will do."

Kreevich began ticking items off on his fingers. "What kind of trouble is Patrick Landis in? He got six hundred bucks from his mother and he hitchhiked East. For more? Did he really just arrive last night, or has he been around longer than that? A kid in big trouble asks his parents for help, and when he doesn't get it goes off his rocker. Knocks off both of them. Today's kids—drug culture—what have you."

"Long shot," Quist said.

"But you might turn up something that would be useful

to Bonham. You need trading material, chum."

"Right."

"The gun," Kreevich said. "Red Landis told you Jim was working on some kind of security system at the Arena. Did that involve his having a gun there? The serial number was filed off, Bonham told you. There'd be no reason for him to have an illegal gun on a perfectly legal job. I assume it wasn't his gun, but find out. Bonham would be grateful. And there's something else that keeps tickling at me."

"Oh?"

"The possibility that the two murders are not connected with each other at all," Kreevich said. His cigarette moved up and down between his lips as he talked. "Wife is brutally murdered. Husband is murdered and draped over his wife's grave. The connection seems certain, and yet—"

"And yet what?" Quist asked.

"These people lived separate lives, as far as we know. Just what Allegra's life was is still unclear. But Landis had a new wife who loves him, believes in him. He had a responsible job at the Arena. Solid citizen after a somewhat wild youth, according to your man Frost at the Arena. Allegra and Landis moved in totally different circles as far as we know. Someone hated her enough to kill her rather brutally. Eight or ten stab wounds suggest rage, hatred. Landis is shot cleanly between the eyes—once. That suggests cold calculation."

"On his wife's grave," Quist said.

"No one says he was shot on his wife's grave," Kreevich said. "The attendant at the cemetery hasn't reported hearing a shot. He just found the body." Kreevich put out a cigarette and poured himself more coffee. "If I plan to kill a man the first problem I have is how to dispose of the body. Yesterday's paper, if I am Landis's killer, supplies me with a perfect notion. I kill him, sit on the body till after dark, and then take it out to the cemetery and try to make it look like a suicide;

give it a connection that doesn't exist."

"Thinking up ideas like that makes it fortunate that you aren't a killer," Quist said.

"Don't brush it too far aside," Kreevich said. "Insisting that the two murders are connected may take you and Bonham both up a dead-end street. You both have two key questions to answer. Who was making love to Allegra the night she was murdered, and where was Jim Landis yesterday morning when he was supposed to be at the funeral? The answers could lead you in two totally different directions. You don't have to tell Bonham how you know Allegra was making love to someone that night. He knows that and so does everyone else who reads the papers. She was prepared, she'd had it, and she was killed later."

Quist nodded slowly. "And what do I hope to get from Bonham in return for what I may be able to give him?" he asked.

"He might tell you if they found any love letters in Allegra's cottage from someone who signed himself 'Y.' " Kreevich's smile was grim. "Bonham is a bulldog kind of a cop, chum. If he found those letters he'll keep at it till he finds out who Y is. In that case your friend Andrew is standing on the edge of a very steep cliff. He might not even be able to get himself elected dogcatcher, let alone a United States Senator."

At ten o'clock on that Friday morning, after three hours' sleep in his Beekman Place apartment, Quist met with his key people in his office, high above Grand Central Station. There were Dan Garvey, dark and intense, Bobby Hilliard with his young Jimmy Stewart boyishness, and Connie Parmalee, the fabulous secretary with the elegant legs who dreamed that no one knew she was hopelessly in love with her boss. If it hadn't been for Lydia—!

There were no secrets from these people. Quist had

warned Andrew of that in the very beginning.

"We have to be ready to turn off the Crown campaign on Monday morning if we haven't gotten Andrew into the clear," Quist told them after he'd briefed them on the whole story. "That means newspaper, radio, and television advertising canceled, speaking dates canceled, fund-raising committees notified, Women Voters for Crown alerted. We can't move before the last minute without arousing suspicions."

"I can handle the advertising contracts and the speaking dates," Connie said, scribbling shorthand notes on her pad.

"The committees and the Women Voters are my job, I guess," Bobby said.

"And my job," Garvey said sourly, "is to advise you to cancel out now, Julian, drop the whole thing. There's no way in the world Andrew Crown can escape being connected with this mess, even if he's as innocent as Snow White. The minute he makes a public appearance, the minute those newspaper ads with his photograph in them appear, Mrs. Nancy Braden will start screaming bloody murder."

"It won't matter if Bonham has the killer or killers," Quist said. "And if Marjorie Crown is standing solidly and publicly at her husband's side."

"Will she, when she has to be told what Mrs. Braden is screaming about?" Garvey asked.

"I'll tell you Monday," Quist said. "Either she'll be ready to take the truth, or we invent a story she and the public will buy. A story that will explain why Andrew was at the cottage the evening of Allegra's murder."

"He was selling encyclopedias," Garvey muttered.

"Your job is to get out to the Arena," Quist said. "What about the gun? What about the security system his wife says he was working on? Where did he go yesterday morning? Everyone in Cranville knows him. Surely someone must have seen him somewhere."

"Did he have any enemies?" Connie suggested. "Were

there people on the staff at the Arena who hated him enough to want him out of the way?"

"Lydia will be trying to get what she can from Red Landis," Quist said.

"The topless tootsie. The whore with the heart of gold," Garvey said.

"A very nice gal, whatever her past," Quist said. "Connie's right. Gossip at the Arena. There must be tons of it. That's yours to dig for, Dan."

"And what about the dozens of other customers this establishment is supposed to be servicing?" Garvey asked, still edgy. "We just drop their concerns and devote ourselves to Andrew Crown's unfruitful love affair?"

"None of them are in trouble," Quist said. "Andrew is. We have today, Saturday, and Sunday in which to bail him out. Let's not argue about it."

Quist and Garvey drove to the Island in separate cars. Garvey would need his own transportation when he got there. Quist headed the Mercedes for Red Landis's dune cottage. There were dark clouds over the ocean and a strongish wind. Thunderstorm warnings, Quist knew.

Quist carried a suitcase to the front door, which Lydia opened before he reached it.

"A change of clothes for you," Quist said. He smiled at her, refreshed by the sight of her. "They must be yours. I found them in my apartment."

"They better be mine," Lydia said, reaching up to kiss his cheek.

"How is Red doing?" he asked.

Lydia kept him standing out on the front step, pulling the door to behind her. "It's been a rough time," she said. "Cops, reporters. Same questions over and over. Did Landis still have some connection with his ex-wife? Did he have other enemies, business enemies? She patiently gives the same answers; the connection he had with Allegra was that they were the parents of two boys. Allegra had been in touch once or twice when one of the boys had a problem. No, he had no enemies as far as she knows. He never mentioned any quarrels or disagreements with people on the job. He was, as far as she knows, liked—well liked. Yes, he went to Allegra's funeral because he thought the boys would expect him to."

"Only he didn't go to the funeral," Quist said.

"Didn't go?"

Quist repeated Crown's statement. "I'm on my way to check with Mrs. Potter, who is the woman who brought Allegra up. But I think it's pretty safe to assume Jim Landis didn't go to the funeral."

"I don't understand," Lydia said.

"He was either stopped on the way by someone, possibly a man who had killing on his mind, or he never intended to go. Used the funeral as an excuse to be absent from his job."

"And to hide where he was really going from Red!" Lydia said.

"Did he hide things from her? I got the idea from Red they were close, warm. Ask her if he was involved in any kind of business venture outside his job. A long time ago, before he married Allegra, Landis was on the wild side. Gambling, among other things. Sometimes the urge gets revived, even after a long time. Was he betting on the horses? Was he a big loser? If so, he could have been in trouble with loan sharks. Ask Red, gently, about it."

"Yes, of course."

"But not too gently, love. Andrew has about sixty hours left before he has to make a decision." Quist touched her face with his fingers, caressing. "I'm off to see Mrs. Potter, who raised Allegra. Dan's over at the Arena. He may turn up here to talk to Red. Try to persuade her his bark is worse than his bite."

Mrs. Elaine Potter, in her seventies, was a retired schoolteacher. She lived in half of a two-family house on a side street in Cranville. She was not, Quist thought, the Whistler's Mother type. Some older women look at younger men as though they'd never known what men were. Ellie Potter, her white hair cropped short, her aristocratically boned face tanned a leathery brown from much outdoors, looked at her handsome visitor with a kind of restrained pleasure. Men still spelled some kind of excitement for her. She was, Quist thought, like a gourmet who could no longer digest highly spiced foods. She remembered what they tasted like but conceded, without bitterness, that they were no longer for her.

Quist introduced himself and hoped she wouldn't object to some questions about Allegra and Jim Landis. She had been working at a flower bed and she took off her gardening gloves and tossed them in a little basket of tools.

"Come up on the porch, Mr. Quist," she said.

He suspected that her quick, energetic movement concealed joints that ached a little, muscles that weren't as flexible as they had once been. He saw that her long, tapering fingers were swollen at the joints by arthritis. Ellie Potter, however, was not prepared to give in to the infirmities of age.

They sat in wicker armchairs on the porch and Quist went into a song and dance about his connection with the Arena and, therefore, his concern about what had happened to Landis. That also led, of course, to Allegra.

"Poor darling," Mrs. Potter said.

"You brought her up, I understand."

Ellie Potter nodded, and her eyes looked far away into the past. "Mathilda Graves and I grew up together," she said. "She was Allegra's mother. We went to school right here in Cranville. I went on to normal school, Mathilda married Larry Graves. He was in Wall Street, and a very nice fellow. But the pressures of getting rich in the late twenties must have been enormous. He and Mathilda were very gay, and

I guess very rich. Then came 1929 and the crash. Larry was wiped out. The money had all been on paper, as they said in those days. In 1933 they had a baby girl, Allegra, at a time they couldn't really afford it. Larry hadn't found anything, just odd jobs. It was a terrible comedown for him. I married Doug Potter about then." She smiled at Quist. "Doug was most-likely-to-succeed in our senior class. An aircraft engineer. In 1937 things got so bad for the Graveses that Doug and I suggested they spend the summer with us here." She turned her head toward the house. "This was a one-family house then. They accepted and came, Larry, Mathilda, and the baby girl. Allegra was four years old. I enjoyed having the child. Doug and I—hadn't been lucky. But it was a rough summer, because Mathilda confided to me that she had it— the big C, as we called it. She didn't have too much longer. She was desperately worried about Allegra and Larry, how they would make out without her."

Quist wanted to get to his questions, but he thought it wiser to let Ellie Potter tell her story. There might be a lead somewhere in it.

"Mathilda died before the next summer rolled around," Ellie Potter said. "Larry Graves was lost, and Doug and I took on Allegra for another stretch. It was not too hard for the child. She already thought of us as another family. The next four years she was in and out of our house. Larry was drinking, drinking. He tried to keep his child and look for work in a small one-and-a-half-room apartment in Greenwich Village. The drinking got so he'd go off on benders and leave Allegra, who was seven, eight years old, to fend for herself. A neighbor in the apartment, a nice girl working in a downtown office, got to checking, and when she found Allegra was alone she'd phone me, and I'd trudge into town and bring her out here. Larry would show up eventually, penitent and full of promises, and then it would happen all over again. Doug and I thought of a formal adoption. But then—then the roof fell in." Ellie Potter was once more looking down that winding road to the past. "Doug was in the Naval Reserve. He was called up in 1940. He was killed right after Pearl Harbor in the Pacific." It was a remembered pain, but Ellie Potter wasn't maudlin about it. "Having Allegra to occupy my concern was a lifesaver in a way. Then Larry was picked up on a street in New York where he'd collapsed. I guess he didn't have any liver left. At any rate he never came out of it. I wanted Allegra, and there were no close relatives clamoring for her. The courts appointed me her guardian in 1942. She was nine years old, bright, eager, a wonderful child." Ellie Potter looked at Quist. "You're letting me run off at the mouth."

"It's fine with me," Quist said. "Getting to understand Allegra may help me to understand Jim Landis, who is my concern."

Ellie Potter frowned. "The next eight years were special for me. Allegra was a delight, curious about everything, wonderfully alive. She was near the top of her class in school. Her friends, girls and boys, were in and out of the house. I kept thinking that sooner or later I'd get around to having that talk about the birds and the bees. Sex. I didn't. I guess I was old-fashioned about it. Then, when she was seventeen, she hit me with a blockbuster. She was pregnant. The man wasn't one of her school friends. He was Jim Landis, ten years older, with a bad reputation in town. She wasn't of age. There could have been serious consequences for him. But Allegra wouldn't hear of it. She loved him and, while I was recovering from the shock, they were married. I thought it was a relationship that had no chance. But Patrick was born, and Jim seemed to make himself over, got steady work, stopped playing around, stopped gambling. Allegra was a wonderful mother. They had David in the second year. Then came a series of misfortunes for her. Two miscarriages. But I watched the boys grow and thought what a miracle it was.

A solid marriage, both of them seeming to be very much in love as the years went by, more in love than they had been at the start, I thought. Then, eighteen months ago, Allegra came to see me. She was in shock. They were going to be divorced. Jim had taken up with some kind of call girl, a nude dancer in an unsavory place down the Thruway."

"But Landis got the divorce," Quist said.

Ellie Potter was silent for a moment. "I think that gave the wrong impression to some people. I think it was just a matter of convenience. Jim had the money, the time to go to court. They didn't want infidelity as the grounds—on account of the boys. Mental cruelty! Allegra never hurt anyone in her life."

"How do you account for what happened to her, Mrs. Potter?"

The woman let her breath out in a shuddering sigh. "An attractive woman, living alone, no man," she said. "Mr. Bonham, the detective, asked me that. There are all kinds of men around the Braden place, stable hands, grooms, gardeners. Isn't it possible that one of them attacked her, raped her, and when she threatened to expose him, killed her?"

"It's been more than a year since the divorce," Quist said. "Was there a new man in Allegra's life? Did she have a new romance?"

The old woman's eyes narrowed, as if she felt some sort of pain. "I have hardly seen Allegra all this last year," she said. "She was a very proud woman, Mr. Quist. She had her job with Eliot Keyes. She kept busy. I think she saw the divorce as a kind of defeat, it would be painful for her to share it with me. We—we just haven't seen each other this last year. Once or twice, and that a casual meeting in the market or at the library."

Quist changed the subject.

"You were at the funeral yesterday morning, Mrs. Potter?"

"Of course I was there. Allegra was like my own child. She is buried in our plot, next to Doug—my husband."

"Did you speak to Jim Landis?"

"Speak to him?"

"At the funeral."

"I didn't speak to him, Mr. Quist, for the simple reason that he wasn't there. Isn't it amazing what guilt does to a man? He left Allegra for some kind of sex symbol; left her alone, unprotected. He felt so responsible for what happened to her that he killed himself on her grave. It's hard to take in."

It was obvious that Bonham hadn't chosen to convey the facts to Mrs. Potter.

"Did Bonham ask you whether you saw Jim Landis at the funeral?"

"I don't recall that he did," Ellie Potter said. "If he had, I'd have told him. Jim wasn't there."

So now maybe Quist had something to trade.

Time, Andrew Crown's prime enemy, moved on. A killer or killers, unidentified, unsuspected as far as Quist was concerned, hovered somewhere, waiting, watching. Allegra Landis had had a rendezvous with a lover, after which she was killed. Who was the lover? Who was the killer? Were they the same person? Jim Landis had not gone to the funeral. So where had he gone? Who had he met and for what purpose? Why had he been killed? Was there any connection between the two crimes?

Too many questions to answer in too short a time, Quist thought. So you doggedly follow any lead you've got and hope that along the way you will stumble on something that means something. There were two leads Quist felt were important. Allegra had had a lover. It didn't sound like a spur-of-the-moment thing. It sounded like an affair. How secret could she have kept it? "Small town, large gossip,"

Bonham had said. A girl friend might have been a confidante. Someone on the Braden estate might have seen something, talked about it. Not the Bradens themselves. They had seen no constant visitor, no "parade of lovers." Mrs. Potter hadn't heard of a romance. But there could have been whispers, heard by more than one person. How to find those people? Was Bonham already on that trail?

The second lead was Landis. Where had he gone instead of to the funeral to which he had told everyone, including Red, he was going? He was no stranger in Cranville. He would have been noticed that day in particular because of the notoriety attached to the funeral of his ex-wife. Somewhere in town someone must have seen him somewhere. But where to begin looking for that someone?

These were questions Quist asked himself as he drove from Mrs. Potter's back to Red Landis's dune cottage. The threatened storm was beginning to break. Rain spattered against the Mercedes' windshield. The ocean waves below the cottage roared as they broke on the beach. Lightning streaked the sky.

Quist parked his car in front of the cottage, tooted his horn several times, and then ran for the front door. Lydia was there to let him in.

He stood inside the door, blotting at his face and hair with a handkerchief. Beyond them in the room was Red Landis, wearing a large pair of black glasses in white frames.

"I'm not a crybaby," she said to Quist, "but I can't stop crying for some reason. My eyes make me look like Joe Frazier after the fight with Muhammad Ali. That's why the cheaters."

There was no way to answer the unspoken question from Lydia. Had Mrs. Potter verified Jim Landis's absence from the funeral? He could answer it by asking Red about it.

"They've given you some peace at last?" he asked.

"That's the reason for crying so much," Red said. Her

painted lips trembled slightly. "They ask the same things over and over. They won't let up."

"The last batch left about ten minutes ago," Lydia said.

"They keep trying to get me to say that Jim had started up with Allegra again." Red shook her head from side to side, a stubborn insistence. "He hadn't. She was long gone as far as Jim was concerned. He—he had me, Mr. Quist!"

"You wanted first names," he said gently. "It's Julian."

"Thanks, Julian. I mean, a woman knows. He was glad to be free of Allegra. But they keep asking and asking."

"So I have to ask something, too," Quist said. "You see, Red, I've learned that Jim didn't go to Allegra's funeral."

"Didn't go!" She sounded genuinely startled.

"He wasn't there."

"Who told you that? Because I know he was going."

"Mrs. Potter. There weren't many people there, Red. There's no way he could have been there and not been seen by someone who knew him."

"I don't understand," Red said. "He didn't want to go but he thought, on account of the boys—their not being here— he should sort of stand in for them. I thought it was pretty great of him to even think of it. Maybe he changed his mind on the way."

"And didn't check in with you all day? Didn't turn up on his job and didn't let them know he wasn't coming? Something turned him off, Red, or he never meant to go. Was he in some kind of trouble? What about money?"

"We weren't saving anything," Red said. "He kept saying there'd be time for that. But we weren't spending more than he took in." She paused, frowning. "That boy you saw, Patrick, was always in trouble. Writing for money. Once he tried to make a collect phone call but Jim wouldn't accept it. If Jim had done what Patrick asked, we'd have been in real trouble. But Jim said he was a man, he should take care of himself." Again a brief hesitation. "The only time, so far as

I know, that Jim had any contact with Allegra after the divorce, she called to say Patrick needed six hundred bucks. If Jim would put it up, she'd pay him back. Jim said no. If she wanted to help Patrick, she'd have to find it somewhere else. She had rich friends."

"What rich friends?"

"That lawyer she worked for. What's his name? Keyes? The people that let her have that cottage. That Mrs. Braden was a Caldwell. Her old man practically owned this town once. Allegra had people she could turn to."

"So he didn't have money trouble—at least that you know about. He hadn't gone back to gambling?"

"No! He said that was like alcoholism. You couldn't take one drink—you can't make one bet."

"Enemies?"

"I don't know what you're trying to get at, Julian! Sure he had an enemy. The sonofabitch that killed him! How big an enemy can you have?"

"But he hadn't mentioned anyone he was having trouble with? Someone on the job?"

"No." Again her mouth trembled. "He walked out of here yesterday morning as relaxed as you or me. Oh, I think he felt a little queasy about going to the funeral, but no other problems. We—we'd had a great night together. We—" She turned away, shoulders shaken with sobs. She needed to be left alone.

Quist turned to Lydia. "Dan hasn't called?"

"No."

"I've got to try to catch up with Bonham," Quist said. "The time has come to join forces, if he will."

Red focused her black glasses on Quist. "If you're going to see Mr. Bonham, Julian, would you ask him something for me?"

"Of course."

"Mr. Bonham turned over Jim's personal belongings to

me—his wallet with his driver's license, credit cards, and like that; loose money he'd been carrying. But there was something missing."

"Oh?"

"His camera. Jim never went anywhere without a camera."

"What kind of a camera was it?"

"Gee, I don't know, Julian. He had eight or ten. It was his one real extravagance. He kept some of them in his darkroom here in the basement, some in his office at the Arena. He used different ones for different occasions. I didn't keep track of what they were. But he was carrying one when he left yesterday morning, and Mr. Bonham didn't return it to me."

"I'll ask him about it," Quist said.

CHAPTER THREE

Henry Bonham turned out to be not as cold and unapproachable as he'd appeared to be on first meeting. He had come up through the state troopers and later the District Attorney's office. He had learned that impersonal approach to the public—that "Let me see your license, please" approach. As he listened to what Quist had to tell him, he seemed to thaw a little.

"I ought to have my head examined," he said. "I asked for a list of people 'in addition to her family' who were at the funeral." He fumbled in a wire basket on his desk, produced a typed list, and passed it to Quist. "I assumed Landis because everyone said he was going there—the people at the Arena, his wife. My man put Mrs. Potter on the list as 'legal guardian.' He did his job, I didn't do mine."

The list was short. It included Ellie Potter, John Braden, Eliot Keyes, three local newspapermen, the undertaker's crew, the day watchman at the cemetery, two girls who, it appeared, worked in Eliot Keyes's office. Some woman who had been in the cemetery to put flowers on some other grave was a curiosity watcher—a Mrs. Gower. She ran a dress shop in Cranville and hadn't known Allegra.

"Either he never meant to go to the funeral, or he was turned off on the way," Quist said.

Bonham took another piece of paper from his wire basket. "Medical Examiner's report," he said. "Landis's body was found on his ex-wife's grave about nine-thirty in the evening. The ME had it about ten. He estimates Landis had been dead for from ten to twelve hours. That means he was killed in the morning—just before, during, or just after the funeral. That means someone concealed the body all day and into the evening, then took it to the cemetery and planted it on the new grave."

"Where could the body have been hidden?"

Bonham shrugged. "He went somewhere private with someone, maybe willingly, maybe not. If it was someone's house, it would be easy enough to keep the body there till after dark, put it in the trunk of a car, and drive it out to St. Peter's."

"That explains why the night custodian didn't hear a shot. Landis wasn't killed there."

"That's for sure." Bonham took off his glasses and blew on the lens, wiping them with a yellow cleaner-cloth. "When I was at the Landis cottage I noticed a candid photo of you on the wall. You see it?"

"Yes."

"Did Landis ask your permission to take it?"

"No. I didn't know he'd taken it till I saw it there."

Bonham put his glasses on again. "He was a bug on taking candid shots, I'm told. Suppose you were a successful businessman, well married, and someone took a picture of you with some chick you shouldn't have been with? Then someone suggests that it might be worth something to you not to have your wife see that picture."

"Blackmail?"

"Landis must have hundreds of pictures and negatives stashed away somewhere. I suppose we're going to have to go through them—which could take weeks!"

"What about Landis's bank account?" Quist asked. "If he was picking up substantial hunks from time to time—?"

"He has an account in the Cranville bank. It shows nothing irregular. His weekly salary. Of course, he could have other bank accounts. But damn it, Quist, it's just a theory without anything to back it up. It would take a staff of people a long time to go through the prints and negatives, and most likely they wouldn't know what they were looking at. But it occurred to me that you, or some of the people in your outfit, could look at Landis's pictures and you'd probably know who shouldn't be with who. You deal with rich people, famous people, and they're the prime targets for blackmail."

"He may have them catalogued, indexed, somewhere."

"That I can check on," Bonham said.

"Incidentally, Mrs. Landis says a camera is missing. He had one on him when he started out for the funeral. You didn't return it with his other effects."

"There wasn't a camera on him when we found him," Bonham said. "What kind was it?"

"She didn't know. I take it she wasn't interested in photography."

"It might be a big help if we could find it," Bonham said. "How about it? Could you have someone look at the prints and negatives?"

"We could give it a whirl," Quist said. He smiled. "I'll make you a trade."

"What kind of trade?"

"Kreevich thinks we shouldn't try to link the two murders," Quist said, "but I can't help toying with it."

"Landis's killer wanted us to," Bonham said. "He ran some risks to leave the body on Allegra Landis's grave."

"In spite of local gossip," Quist said, "I've listened to Mrs. Potter and Eliot Keyes and they give Allegra very high marks. Hearing what they say, I keep telling myself Allegra wouldn't have been making love with anyone but her ex-husband. He was her man—her only man."

"And he wasn't there. His alibi holds up for that night. He was at the Arena."

"Maybe that alibi should be more thoroughly checked," Quist said. "But maybe she had a lover. Did you find anything in her cottage to suggest that? Love letters, for example?"

"We took the cottage apart, looking for fingerprints, any other thing that would lead us to who was there," Bonham said. "There were no letters, except for a half dozen from her son who's in the army."

"Well, that's that," Quist said, trying not to show his relief. Andrew Crown was safe for the time being, at least. "Have you heard Mrs. Potter's theory that Allegra was attacked by some of the work crew on the Braden estate?"

Bonham nodded slowly. "There are eight men working on the estate," he said. He ticked them off on his fingers. "Two gardeners, two stable hands, a head groom, a trainer, and two exercise boys. They all live on the grounds, sleep in a sort of bunkhouse. Braden has a local woman who cooks for them. They all tend to alibi each other. The kind of alibis I usually buy because they aren't foolproof. Foolproof alibis are usually planned in advance. But Mrs. Potter is thinking rape. We know better. That stable crew and the gardeners might be capable of rape, but Allegra Landis apparently chose her man that night. I also get the picture that she was a rather fastidious person. I don't think she'd have chosen any one of those eight guys." Bonham brought the palm of his hand down hard on his desk. "If we could just identify and locate the man Mrs. Braden saw!"

"That's your best shot?"

"What else, for God sake," Bonham said. He put the reports back in his wire basket. "I understand you're going to handle Andrew Crown's campaign for the Senate."

Quist felt his heart pound against his ribs. "Yes."

"I'm going to vote for him," Bonham said. "I'm sick of professional politicians. It's time for some new blood."

The thunderstorm had left the air fresh and cool. Late afternoon sunlight glistened on wet foliage. It was time, Quist thought, to catch up with Dan Garvey at the Arena. The sun was about to go down on the second day and they were no closer to answers that would put Andrew Crown in the clear than they had been at the start.

Bonham's theory about Landis as a blackmailer was interesting but not based on anything solid. It could provide a motive for someone, but who? Lydia and some of the people at the Quist offices could be turned loose on hundreds, maybe even thousands, of photographs and negatives. They might come up with something compromising if they were enormously lucky. But proof that would lead to Landis's killer? One in a million, Quist thought.

Bonham had nothing on the butchering of Allegra except Nancy Braden's "agitated man" who was, unfortunately, Andrew. There wasn't time to speculate about Allegra's love life or Jim Landis's possible criminal behavior. They had to find solid evidence, and in a hurry. So far there wasn't a shred of it.

As he approached the Arena, Quist found himself blocked from entering the parking lot by the exiting of thousands of cars from the area. He realized that the circus matinee must just have concluded. A state trooper, directing traffic, finally squeezed him across the flow of cars and into the lot. It took him a good ten minutes to edge his way into the employees' space. Once again he made his way through the back corridors to Ted Frost's office. Once again the young Arena manager was checking out on gate receipts. He gave Quist a kind of harried grin.

"The circus never seems to lose its charm," he said. "Full house for every performance. But I sure will be glad when we stop catering to kids. They're a handful."

"I can imagine."

"Well, only three more performances," Frost said. "Tonight, and two tomorrow. Then we move 'em out in the middle of the night and transform the place into an ice palace. Olympic figure skating trials Sunday afternoon and evening. No rest for the weary."

"Do you know if Dan Garvey is somewhere around?" Quist asked.

"I assume he is," Frost said. "At least he didn't stop by to say good-bye or return my key if he has left."

"Your key?"

"He wanted to have a look at Jim Landis's office. Incredible about Landis, isn't it?"

"Is there a way to check it out? It's important for me to make contact with Dan."

Frost moved to a large keyboard at one side of his office. Hundreds of keys hung from little brass hooks. "Key's not here," he said. "I thought he might have dropped it off when I was moving around somewhere. I'll call Landis's office." He picked up the phone on his desk and dialed three numbers on it. After a reasonable wait he put down the phone. "I guess he isn't there. No answer. You know, I used to go to Yankee Stadium every Sunday afternoon when he was playing. I still say he was better than Gale Sayers or O. J. Simpson."

"He might not answer the phone," Quist said. "He wouldn't expect it to be for him, would he?"

"I suppose not."

"How do I find the office?"

"It's one floor below ground level," Frost said. "That's where the dressing rooms for performers and players are located. Take the fire stairs at the end of the corridor outside and go down two flights. Turn left and the office is about three doors down on your left. Landis's name is on the door. I'll get someone to guide you if you want. I have to stay with these figures before the accountants check in with me."

"I can find it," Quist said.

"Tell Dan not to forget the key," Frost said.

"Will do."

Quist had once been given a guided tour of the Arena and recalled his amazement at its underground labyrinth: offices, dressing rooms, ice making machines, storage places for board floors, for small tractors, ice sweeping machines, basketball hoops, boxing rings, and literally hundreds of other pieces of equipment that weren't self-explanatory. There were huge service elevators that could lift trucks, animals, whole teams of players for any sport. On still a lower level were air conditioning and heating machinery, a mammoth generator that provided the Arena with its own electrical power. Quist thought of the place as being a self-contained little city with its restaurants, bars, beauty parlors and barbershops, sauna baths, squash and handball courts, the Sponsors' Club, even a hospital.

Quist went down the fire stairs to the first level below the ground. He was immediately aware of air conditioning, freshened air. There were, of course, no windows. The corridor he found himself in was lighted by fluorescent fixtures.

He came face to face with a clown, grotesque makeup still on his face but his costume missing. He was dressed in an undershirt and slacks. Quist guessed the clowns didn't remove their elaborate makeup between afternoon and evening performances.

He found the office he was looking for. There was a frosted glass top to the door and on it was printed in gold letters, ARENA CATERING SERVICE, JAMES LANDIS.

There was no light showing from the other side of the frosted glass. Quist tried the door and found it open. He stepped into darkness. Instinctively he reached out with his right hand, searching for a light switch. He found it, pushed it down. The fluorescents blinked and then turned the office into daylight.

Quist stood perfectly still, staring at wild disorder. Filing cabinets were open, their contents scattered on the floor. The desk top was littered with papers. A wall safe stood open.

Then Quist's muscles tightened. Protruding from behind the desk were two feet, encased in brown shoes, toes pointing to the ceiling. Quist moved quickly around the desk and looked down on Dan Garvey's ashen face, smeared with blood.

Quist's lips moved, but no sound came from them. He knelt down and his fingers searched for a pulse in Garvey's throat. Without moving his friend, Quist could only guess at what must be a brutal wound at the back of his head.

There was an all-too-faint pulse.

Quist turned to the phone on the disordered desk. He shuffled papers, searching for something that would show him intercom numbers. He just tried dialing "O" and an impersonal switchboard voice asked, "How can I help you?"

"An emergency in the catering office," Quist said in a voice he didn't recognize as his own. "The house doctor, please. And hurry."

He knelt down beside Garvey again and took one of his friend's ice-cold hands in his.

"Keep in there, chum," he said softly. "You've got to keep in there pitching."

The next stretch of time was like a nightmare to Quist when he tried to recall it, a nightmare composed of strange sights and smells and unbearable tensions.

He knelt beside Garvey, talking to him as though he could hear, reassuring him, demanding courage from him. He remembered a sizzling string of profanity directed at a doctor who seemed to take so long in coming. Sonofabitch had probably stopped somewhere on the way for a short beer. It turned out later that the doctor had actually arrived within minutes, as quickly as it could possibly have been managed.

Quist remembered the sick sweet smell of Garvey's blood, other smells that must have been indigenous to the room itself. Was it chemicals of some sort? Had something been burned in the office? He wanted to search the place for traces of the person who had assaulted Garvey, to identify the odors, but he couldn't bring himself to leave Garvey's side, to let go of his hand. There was another all-pervading odor that he finally identified as coming from the circus animals quartered on the level below this one.

Then the doctor came, young, wearing a white coat and carrying a black medical bag.

"What took you so goddamned long?" Quist heard himself shouting.

The doctor gave him a cool, assessing look and went about his business, which was Garvey.

There was a quick examination and then the doctor went to the phone. His voice was calm, unexcited. "We need a stretcher in a hurry," he said to whomever he'd called. "Call County Hospital. We need an ambulance to take in an emergency. Have them alert Dr. Zukor. It looks like a skull fracture."

111

"Isn't there anything you can do for him, Doctor?" Quist asked.

"Pulse very weak," the young doctor said. "Isn't this man's name Garvey, public relations for the Arena? I've seen him around."

Quist told him yes, and that he was Dan's business partner.

"How did it happen? Looks like a cyclone struck this place." The doctor was preparing some kind of an injection for Garvey.

"I don't know. I found him this way."

"You called the police?"

"Not yet."

"Well, for God sake, man! We'll be lucky if this doesn't turn out to be a murder. Call. Call now, while I give him this shot. Dial O for an outside line."

He felt like an automaton as he dialed and asked information to get him Henry Bonham's office. He saw the doctor give him a surprised look. Bonham wasn't in until Quist gave his name and insisted it was an emergency. Then Bonham came on the line. Quist spelled it out, short and sweet.

"Don't move anything or touch anything. I'll be there in fifteen minutes," Bonham said.

"They're taking Dan to the hospital. I'm going with him."

"Then lock the office. Make sure no one goes in. Get back to me when you can."

Quist put his finger down on the cutoff button. "How do I dial for Frost?" he asked the doctor.

"Two-eight-O," the doctor said.

Frost sounded shocked, but said he would be there directly. The doctor was showing signs of impatience. Finally two men wearing Arena ushers' uniforms arrived with a stretcher. The doctor gave instructions for moving Garvey onto the stretcher. He himself stayed at Garvey's head, holding it still as the men lifted Garvey gently.

"We'll take him up to the street level and wait for the ambulance there," the doctor said.

Frost arrived just as they were carrying Garvey out into the hall. Quist told him the office was to be locked until Bonham arrived. Then he followed the stretcher toward the elevator at the end of the hall. Later he remembered strange faces, his friend the clown, an enormous fat woman standing in an open doorway, a girl wearing leotards with long golden hair hanging below her shoulders who shrank back against the wall as they carried the stretcher past her. Then the low humming sound as the elevator, big enough to carry two trucks, lifted them up to the street level.

There was a small emergency room just off the Arena lobby and they took Garvey there. They'd hardly arrived when they heard the ambulance siren in the parking area. The doctor sent one of the stretcher-bearers with instructions.

"You want to ride with us?" the doctor asked.

"I'll follow," Quist said. "I'll need wheels once I know how things are."

"You might as well face it," the doctor said. "Things are bad, Mr. Quist."

Then there was a wild ride through traffic and out to the Thruway, Quist's Mercedes hanging onto the blinking taillights of the ambulance. A speed cop saw them, started after them, and then realized that Quist was with the ambulance.

At the hospital Quist stood by the ambulance as Garvey was lifted out. The young doctor took time to instruct him.

"Go to the fifth floor waiting room," he said. "They'll take him straight to surgery. Tell them at the desk I sent you. Dr. Zukor's case."

"You know, Doctor, I haven't even bothered to ask your name," Quist said.

"Corbett." The doctor started to turn away.

"In spite of all my shouting at you, Dr. Corbett, I know

how quick and efficient you've been. I'm grateful."

"My job," Corbett said, and followed the ambulance stretcher into the emergency entrance.

Hospitals are alike everywhere, Quist thought. On the fifth floor a nurse at the desk showed him where he could wait. There were the little tinkling bells, the antiseptic smells, the squawk box that perpetually asked for Dr. This or Dr. That to report somewhere.

"It may be a long time," the nurse said. "There's a coffee machine at the end of the hall."

It was growing dark outside the windows with a sprinkling of community lights, like fireflies. Quist found that he was coming out of the kind of daze that had engulfed him since the moment he'd found Dan in that office, and that it was being replaced by a slow-burning almost painful rage. Dan had gone to that office, probably hoping to find something there that would answer some of the questions about Landis they needed to know. He had either surprised someone there or been surprised himself after he'd arrived, someone totally ruthless. Whoever that someone was, Quist meant to find him and repay him in kind. It was quite possible neither Dan nor his attacker had been seen or noticed. The circus matinee had been in full swing when Dan had gone down there. The circus performers using the dressing rooms on that level had probably all been up above in the main arena. The attacker had brutally beaten Dan, a Dan caught entirely by surprise. Garvey, an athlete, always in top condition, actually a karate expert, couldn't have been taken so easily without total surprise. Quist imagined someone in the office, hearing Dan's key in the lock, hiding, waiting for Garvey to sit down at Landis's desk, then creeping up behind him and bludgeoning him. It was the only way it could have happened to a man of Dan's fighting skills. The attacker had then gone on with his search, tearing the office apart. Gone on? He couldn't have started when Dan arrived or Dan would have been instantly alerted, would never have sat down calmly at Landis's desk, turning his back on the unknown.

It could be a long time, the nurse had said. Quist decided he'd better call Lydia and tell her what had happened. He went back to the desk, looked up the Landis phone number in the book, and dialed the number from the pay phone booth near the elevators. No answer. He glanced at his watch and saw that it was going on eight o'clock. The two girls had probably gone out somewhere for dinner.

When a friend is in trouble you remember so many things about him, little things, funny things, warm and important things. Quist remembered the day Dan Garvey had come to his office six years ago. He had been a star running back on a local pro-football team, cut down by a knee injury. He was a proud man, dark and handsome, daring Quist to feel sorry for him. He had an idea for a special kind of television sports show. He wanted Quist's advice and, hopefully, his help. Quist had handled quite a few top figures in the world of sports. Garvey was asking to be handled, promoted, to have an image built for him. They had played around with Garvey's idea and Quist didn't think too much of it. But he liked Garvey. He suggested that Garvey become a member of the firm, dealing with other sports figures. He turned out to be something of a genius at it. He became a close, warm friend. There were funny things about Dan. It was only by accident that Quist learned that he had a Phi Beta Kappa key hidden away in his handkerchief drawer. It was as if he was ashamed of scholastic achievement. Women swooned over Garvey and he liked women. Almost instantly he joined the firm he saw Lydia, decided she was for him, and discovered, to his enormous embarrassment, that she belonged to Quist—and vice versa. He was quick to disagree, but when he was outvoted he gave everything he had to whatever the project was. They had shared danger together, and Quist had never felt so secure as when he and Dan were fighting shoulder to

115

shoulder. Quist knew that he loved the man and cherished their friendship. *This just had to work out!*

It seemed to have been endless hours, was actually two, when a doctor in a green operating suit came into the area where Quist was waiting.

"Mr. Quist? I'm Dr. Zukor." And before Quist could ask a question the doctor held up white, silencing hands. "I can only say—maybe. The damage is severe. Skull fracture—how much worse I don't know yet."

"Worse?"

"Brain damage."

"Can he talk? We don't know yet what happened to him."

"Talk? We'll be lucky if he can ever talk. Certainly not soon."

"His chances—an honest guess, Doctor?"

"Say two in ten," the doctor said. "I'm sorry I can't be more optimistic."

"I'd like to stay with him, at least until he comes to," Quist said. "He should know that he just hasn't been dumped here."

"My dear sir," the doctor said with exaggerated patience, "he isn't going to 'come to,' as you put it, for a long time. It will be a miracle if he can recognize you forty-eight hours from now. Go home. You look dead on your feet. Where can we reach you if—if there is any reason to reach you?"

"I don't know yet where I'm staying. They'll know at the Island Arena when I know. Also Henry Bonham in the prosecutor's office. Thank you, Doctor."

"You could pray a little—if you believe in it," Dr. Zukor said.

Quist's eyes felt inflamed and hot as he drove the Mercedes back toward the Arena. Anger was burning him up. He knew he was close to physical exhaustion, but he also knew that rest was impossible. Bonham must have come up with something by now, a lead to follow. All he wanted was to get on the track of Garvey's attacker and run him to earth. Time for rest after that.

The night performance of the circus was over, but the employees' parking area was loaded with cars, including two State Police cruisers. Frost's office was locked, and Quist headed down the fire stairs to Landis's office on the first sub-level.

Cleaning crews were at work in the main Arena. In the corridor outside Landis's office a state trooper stopped him.

"My name is Quist," Quist said. "Is Bonham still here? He'll vouch for me. I'm the one who found the victim. I've just come from the hospital."

The trooper waved him in. The little office was crowded with working police, photographers, a fingerprint man. Bonham, Frost, and a captain of troopers were in a corner of the room, watching.

"How is he?" Bonham asked.

"Touch and go," Quist said in a flat voice. "Chances less than good."

"Damn! He can't talk yet?"

"If ever," Quist said. "What have you found?"

"Not a hell of a lot," Bonham said. "This is Captain Roark, in charge of the local barracks."

Quist and the trooper nodded to each other.

"There are dozens of fingerprints, but God knows who they belong to. Whoever it was went through the office from top to bottom, burned a lot of stuff in the metal wastebasket, mostly photos and negatives."

"Then he found what he was looking for," Quist said.

Fluorescent lights glittered against the lenses of Bonham's glasses. "I don't think so," he said. "I'm more sold than ever on the blackmail theory we discussed. I think he was looking for specific pictures and negatives. He certainly didn't find them right away, or why tear the place apart? Garvey must have walked in on him while he was searching."

"Not that," Quist said. "Dan is a very tough cookie. If he'd walked into the office looking halfway like this, he'd never have been caught off guard. He was sitting at the desk and someone struck him from behind. I figure the man was already in here, heard Dan's key in the lock, and hid. That had to be before he'd even started to search. He clobbered Dan and then began his search. He must have been frantic to get it done, wondering if someone would come looking for Dan."

"Sounds logical," Bonham said. "But I don't think he found what he was looking for. He must have been in a hurry. So he burned every picture and negative he could lay hands on, just to be sure he hadn't overlooked what he was after."

"How did he get into that wall safe?" Quist asked.

"It wasn't forced," Bonham said. "A lot of people are foolish about safes. Landis probably had the combination written down somewhere. We'll probably find it in this mess."

Quist looked at Frost. "What did Landis keep in the safe?"

"Money taken at the concession stands during the evening performance," Frost said.

"So was money stolen?"

Frost shook his head. "He wasn't coming in yesterday morning because of the funeral, so he turned over Thursday night's receipts to me."

"Our boy was just looking for pictures," Bonham said. "He probably figured important ones, blackmail bait, would be locked away. The safe would be the first place he'd look. I figure they weren't there and then he began a hysterical search of the rest of the place."

"All the time Garvey was lying there on the floor," Frost said. He sounded sick.

"You find a weapon?" Quist asked.

"No. Dr. Corbett thinks it could have been a gun butt. He thinks Garvey was hit several times—by someone frenzied," Bonham said.

Roark spoke for the first time. "I was just saying when you came in, Quist, that if our man didn't find what he was looking for here, there might be some other place he'd go to hunt. I was about to suggest we take a look at Landis's house."

Quist felt his blood turning slowly to ice water.

"Oh, my God!" he said.

"What is it?" Bonham asked.

"Miss Morton is there with Mrs. Landis," Quist said. "I called them a couple of times, hours ago. There was no answer and I decided they'd gone out to dinner somewhere."

"Try them again," Bonham said.

"You try them!" Quist said.

He turned and ran out of the office.

PART THREE

CHAPTER ONE

The dune cottage was dark. It was after midnight and the two girls could have gone to bed. Every instinct Quist had told him that wasn't possible. He parked the Mercedes so that its headlights were focused on the front door of the cottage. His mouth felt painfully dry as he got out of the car and ran up the path.

He pounded on the door. There was no response. He pounded with both fists. He tried the door and found it locked. He stepped back a pace or two and threw a shoulder block against it. It was a strong door, made to resist an attempt at forcing.

Quist remembered that around the other side of the cottage was a sort of deck outside the picture window that overlooked the ocean. He went around the corner and vaulted up onto the deck. There were a couple of deck chairs, a white painted iron table, and two white painted iron garden chairs. There were two ash trays and what looked like a box for cigarettes on the table. Quist swept them off and lifted the heavy table, balanced himself for an instant, and hurled it against the picture window. The glass shattered and Quist felt a stab of pain on the back of the hand he'd raised to cover his face.

He stepped over and through jagged spears of glass and into the living room. He was shouting now.

"Lydia! Red!"

No answer. He felt his way along the wall, stumbling over something that felt like an overturned chair, feeling for a light switch. He found it and the room was lighted. He stood there, back against the wall, his breath whistling between his teeth. Someone had torn this room apart just as thoroughly as Landis's office.

"Lydia! Red! Where are you?"

He knew there was going to be no answer but he had to try for one. He headed for the kitchen, turning on the light there. Another shambles, pots and pans scattered about, two glass jars that looked as if they'd contained flour and sugar overturned, contents spilled out on the floor.

He made for the two bedrooms. They had been torn apart too, bedding thrown off the beds, mattresses slit open, bureau drawers emptied. The whole place was tornado-struck.

Then Quist remembered that Jim Landis had a darkroom in the basement. He found a light switch at the head of the cellar stairs and he went down. Off in the distance he heard a police siren. Bonham and the state troopers were close by.

He found himself in a small utility room that contained an oil burner and a hot water tank. To the right was a door that probably led into the darkroom. He was aware of a familiar smell. Burned film, he thought.

He opened the darkroom door, found a light switch on the wall. The tornado had struck here too, but Quist scarcely noticed.

"Oh, God!" he said.

The two girls were there, trussed up like Thanksgiving turkeys. There was adhesive tape around ankles, around

124

wrists, and across mouths. Two pairs of wide, frightened eyes stared at him.

Quist heard himself indulging in a grotesque giggle. It was a sort of hysterical relief. They were alive!

He got to Lydia first. "This is going to hurt," he said.

He took the edge of the tape over her mouth and gave it a quick jerk. There were tears in her eyes but she, too, was laughing.

"What kept you?" she asked.

It had happened early in the evening, not long after dark. Red Landis had prepared a light supper for them and they had been sitting in the living room going over and over the double tragedy. Red couldn't get away from it, couldn't stop asking the why of it. There had been a knock at the door. They'd thought "another reporter." Red had slipped into the bedroom and Lydia had gone to the door.

"There was this man, wearing a ski mask and pointing what looked to me like a cannon right at my face!" Lydia said.

She was sitting on the couch next to Quist, leaning back against his shoulder, his arm holding her close. Red Landis, pale and still shaken, sat in the other corner of the couch wearing her black glasses in their white frames. Bonham and Captain Roark faced them. Outside the windows flashlights blinked in the night. Troopers were searching the grounds and the beach for some trace of the man who had made prisoners of the two girls.

It had taken time to get the half-hysterical girls in some kind of shape to talk. Bonham and Roark had arrived in the darkroom in time to help Quist free them from their bonds. Lydia had given a vague description of the man in the ski mask: dark clothes, the dark mask, slim and wiry. He was terribly strong, Lydia thought. He had handled both girls roughly, forcing them down into the darkroom. He had held the gun on them, ordering Lydia to tape Red's ankles, wrists, and mouth. Then he had literally thrown Lydia down onto the floor and taped her up himself.

"His voice?" Bonham had asked.

"It was muffled," Lydia said. "The mask—"

Quist insisted on no more questions until they got pulled together. They had gone up into the cottage, Quist holding onto Lydia as though she might vanish. Red was in tears as she saw the destruction.

"My lovely house," she said, choking on sobs. "Oh, my God, my lovely house!"

Quist went into the bedroom area with them. There he had a moment to be alone with his woman. He held her close. He could feel her trembling.

"You're all right?"

"I'm fine, now that you're here," she said.

Quist went back into the living room and poured two stiff drinks for the girls. Bonham and Roark were going over the place.

"As soon as possible," Bonham said to Quist.

"You want facts and not hysterics, don't you?" Quist said.

Finding Lydia in one piece had acted like a shot of adrenalin on Quist. He couldn't let her get beyond his reach. While Lydia "put on a new face" Quist told her about Garvey. She was shocked.

"You think it may have been the same man who was here?" she asked.

"Who else?"

"He was like a madman searching for what had to be a picture of some sort," Lydia said. "He went through files of developed photos, throwing each one into a big metal basket there in the darkroom. Then negatives, holding each one up to the light. He made sounds, inarticulate sounds, as though he was talking to himself. Desperate sounds. Each negative in the basket. Then—then he set fire to the lot. My God, Julian, I thought he was going to burn down the place with Red and me in it!"

The cottage hadn't burned down, though Captain Roark found scorch marks on the ceiling of the darkroom. It had been very close to sending the whole place up in flames.

Finally the girls were ready to face Bonham and Roark, and Quist took them out into the living room. Lydia and Red couldn't answer key questions. They couldn't give the attacker a face, a voice. Lydia reported again on his strength, the violent way he had thrown her to the floor. She remembered that he had been wearing gloves, black gloves.

"So no fingerprints," Bonham said. His cold pale eyes were narrowed. "Mrs. Landis, did this man ask you any questions? He was looking for something in your house. You'd think he might ask you where to find it."

Red shook her head slowly. "He didn't ask us anything. He just—just waved his gun at us and—and made us go down to the darkroom. He seemed to know where it was. Then he made Lydia tape my feet and wrists and—and my mouth! Then he did the same thing to her. He never asked anything."

Quist could feel Lydia's body tighten. "He set fire to the stuff in the metal basket and the flames—I was sure he was going to leave us to be burned to death. The flames shot up! But—but then we could hear him going over the house upstairs, tearing things apart. At last he went away and the fire subsided. Then it seemed forever before Julian found us. We couldn't move. We couldn't do anything. I couldn't help free Red, and she couldn't help me."

Bonham lit a cigarette. "He didn't find what he wanted at the Arena, or why come here? And it would seem he didn't find it here either. Can you suggest, Mrs. Landis, anyplace anywhere your husband might hide something he didn't want found?"

127

"I can't think of any," Red said. "And I don't understand. Why would he want to hide pictures he'd taken? Because that creep was obviously looking for a picture."

"Or pictures," Bonham said. "Your husband must have taken a picture or pictures of someone that were worth killing him to get them back. Obviously this person didn't get them from your husband so he runs all kinds of risks to find them at the Arena and then here."

"It just doesn't make any sense to me," Red said.

"We think your husband may have tried to blackmail someone with compromising photos," Roark said.

"Blackmail! That's crazy!" Red said.

"You say your husband always carried a camera with him," Roark said.

"He never went anywhere without one," Red said. "I used to get teed off with him because he was always stopping to take pictures of someone or something."

"Expensive hobby," Roark said. "There were two cameras down in the darkroom, and I know a little something about costs. There is a Nikon, 35mm, Japanese-made, must have cost him seven hundred bucks. And a Rolleiflex that must have gone a thousand."

Red looked surprised. "That much?"

"You saw him leave yesterday morning, supposedly going to the funeral. Was he carrying a camera then?"

"He always carried a case—leather, with a strap over one shoulder."

"So there was a third camera," Roark said, "since he couldn't have been carrying either of those in the darkroom. He never came back here. That makes three. Were there any more? Did he keep any at the Arena?"

"I honestly don't know." Red said. Her voice rose, as if she was close to cracking up again. "Why does it matter?"

"Because he wasn't carrying a camera when he was found," Roark said. "He lost one somewhere, left it somewhere. If we could find it it might help us. But we don't know what we're looking for."

At that moment they heard the sound of two gunshots outside the cottage, some shouting, a third gunshot. Roark headed for the front door, drawing his gun on the way. Quist's first instinct was to protect Lydia. He rolled to his right, covering her body with his.

"Down, Red—on the floor!" he called out.

Roark had reached the door and opened it.

"It's okay, Captain, we got him!" a voice shouted from some distance away.

Two troopers came up the path dragging someone between them. The man, handcuffed, was projected into the living room. A trickle of blood ran from the corner of his mouth, apparently the result of a scuffle with the troopers.

It was Patrick Landis, the bearded son of two murdered parents.

The troopers had found young Landis hiding in a clump of bushes at the rear of the cottage. He wasn't armed. There was no sign of the ski mask that the man who had attacked the two girls and wrecked the cottage had worn. Of course they hadn't had an opportunity to search the area, and it was a difficult task in the dark. The gun and the mask could have been discarded anywhere on the grounds, and Roark ordered his men to search for them.

"The man with the gun and mask finished his search here hours ago," Quist said. "Why would he still be hanging around—waiting to be caught?"

Patrick Landis kept looking from one to the other of them, his eyes wide and wild-looking. Quist remembered wondering about drugs the first time he'd seen him.

"So, Mr. Landis—?" Bonham asked quietly.

"This is my father's house," Patrick said in a high, harsh voice. "What am I guilty of, trespassing? What's all this crap about a gun and a mask?''

"We ask the questions," Bonham said. "What were you doing here?"

Patrick moistened bloody lips. His hands were locked behind his back. "This is my father's house!" he said. "There may be things here that belong to me. I—I was waiting for a chance to look for them."

"At one o'clock in the morning?"

Patrick glared at Red, his stepmother. "She'd never have let me look. I thought—after she'd gone to bed—"

"How did you propose to get in?"

"I—I have a key."

"No!" Red said. She sounded frightened.

"From way back, while my mother and father were still together—before *she* crawled into his bed!" He jerked his head toward Red.

"Where is the key?" Bonham asked.

"In my pants pocket."

Roark went over to Patrick and started to slip his hand into the boy's trouser pocket. Patrick kicked out and caught Roark squarely on the shin. The trooper captain doubled over for an instant, his teeth gritted. Then he straightened up, looked steadily at Patrick, and knocked him flat with a right cross to the jaw.

There was a little cry from Red, and Quist could feel Lydia's fingernails bite into his arm. Roark bent down, fumbled in the boy's pocket and produced a ring with three keys on it. He went over to the front door and tried one of them.

"This one works," he said. He came back to Patrick, who still lay on his back turning his head from one side to the other, moaning. He took Patrick by the back of his collar and yanked him up to his feet. "Don't try anything like that on me again," he warned.

The boy laughed, hysterically, and raised a knee toward Roark's groin. He didn't connect this time, but Roark did

130

with a smashing blow to Patrick's mouth. Patrick went down and lay very still.

"I think we've had about enough of that, Roark," Bonham said.

"Sonofabitch!" Roark said, rubbing his knuckles. "Something's happened to a whole generation of young people—think we're the enemy, for God sake!"

"I don't think he's the man we're looking for," Bonham said. "Like Quist asked, why would he wait around here for hours to be caught?"

"But what did he want?" Red asked, her voice unsteady. "There wasn't anything of his here. Everything that belonged to Allegra and the boys was cleaned out of here long ago. Jim didn't want anything here that would remind him of any of them."

"Are you just going to let him lie there?" Lydia asked, anger near the surface.

Roark and Bonham lifted the boy and stretched him out on the couch. Lydia went into the kitchen and came back with a basin of water and a towel. She wiped at the bleeding mouth and then bathed his whole face with it. Patrick moaned and tried to move.

"Does he have to have those handcuffs on," Lydia asked, "or aren't there enough of you to handle him?"

"Now look here, Miss Morton—" Roark began.

"Take off the cuffs," Bonham said.

Roark controlled his own anger, turned Patrick onto one side and unlocked the cuffs. Then he sat the moaning boy upright and rubbed his hands to get the circulation going. Patrick's eye blinked and he found himself looking straight at Roark.

"Take it easy, Landis," Bonham said. "We can play bounce-the-ball all day if you insist."

Roark waited almost hopefully, Quist thought, for the boy to strike out at him. He didn't. His inflamed eyes filled with tears and he leaned his head back against the couch. It was a surrender of some sort.

Quist looked at Bonham and got an unspoken permission to talk to Patrick.

"The police have two murders on their hands, Patrick, and a murderous assault on a friend of mine who was in your father's office. A man looking for some pictures your father had taken. He came here later, armed, wearing a ski mask, tied up Mrs. Landis and Miss Morton, and went on searching for whatever your father had he wanted. We just found them a little while ago—the girls. It seems probable this man killed your father to get what he wanted. The troopers were looking for some sign of him in the grounds when they found you. They handled you roughly because they thought you might be a killer."

"Bastards!" Patrick muttered.

"We have to know what you were doing here, if you saw anything, if you can help us," Quist said. "The whole Landis family may be his target, you know. You could be next. He doesn't wait to ask questions."

"He's too late to worry about me," the boy said bitterly. "Someone else is going to beat him to it."

Nobody spoke. They all waited, watching him.

"There's a contract out on me," Patrick said.

"Oh, boy!" Roark said. He sounded disgusted. "What is this, some kind of television melodrama. A contract!"

"Tell us about it," Quist said quietly.

All the fight had gone out of Patrick. "Why not?" he said bitterly. "It isn't going to make any difference whether you know or not."

"What were you really doing here?" Bonham asked. "Mrs. Landis says there was nothing of yours here in the cottage."

The boy's mouth twitched at a corner. "Money," he said. "My father had some money for me. If he didn't have it on

132

him when he was killed, I thought it must be here."

"Money that belonged to you?" Red said. "That's crazy! Jim always turned you down when you asked for money."

"You were talking about a contract," Roark said. "Let's not get away from that."

"Let him tell it his own way," Quist said.

A quick glance from Patrick suggested gratitude. "I—I left Cranville almost two years ago," he said. "About six months before my mother and father were divorced. I couldn't stay here any more. You see, she—Allegra—was having an affair with someone."

"Who?" Bonham asked sharply. It sounded like the first real lead he'd had.

"I don't know," Patrick said. "I could guess, of course, but I don't know for sure."

"So guess," Bonham said.

"That lawyer," Patrick said.

For a moment Quist felt his muscles tighten. Andrew Crown? But if Andrew had told the truth, he hadn't known Allegra two years ago.

"What lawyer?" Bonham persisted.

Patrick shrugged. "The one she worked for—part-time in those days. Mr. Keyes. It's only a guess."

"How did you know about it?" Bonham could smell answers.

"I—I came home one evening and she was making out with someone in her bedroom. It—it turned me off. I felt sick about it."

"How do you know it wasn't your father?" Quist asked.

"Because I'd just left him at the Arena. I knew I had to go away somewhere. I couldn't tell my father, and I couldn't stay here looking at Allegra every day, knowing she was putting out for someone."

"You called your mother by her first name?" Roark asked.

133

He was taking notes.

"Yes." Patrick's voice was unsteady. "We used to be very close."

"But this affair changed things?" Quist asked.

"It changed everything," Patrick said. "The next day I faced her with it. She wouldn't tell me what I wanted to know—who the man was. She wouldn't tell me why. She said someday I might understand. So—I told her I had to go away. She cried about it—but she understood. She gave me a couple of hundred bucks, all the bread she had."

"What reason did you give your father for leaving?" Quist asked.

"He didn't ask why. He didn't care. He just said goodbye —and not to send him any S O S's if I got in trouble."

"You didn't get on with him?"

"I hated his guts!" Patrick said.

"But you came here to find some money he had for you?" Roark asked.

"Let him tell it his way!" Quist said, his voice rising.

It came tumbling out of the boy then; all the frustrations and angers and disillusionments that were part of his world and his friends' world. An immoral war, a corrupt government, the blaming of youth for the cynical climate their elders had created, dissent a crime; those were the things that had turned off Patrick Landis and so many others of his generation. There were no long-range goals. As a small boy Patrick had wanted to be a fireman. Now there was nothing he wanted except to live through today, take what came his way, right or wrong. Family had once meant something to him. Now his mother had destroyed that for him.

So Patrick took off for anywhere, with two hundred bucks in his pocket and a bitter taste in his mouth. He wound up in Texas. He did odd jobs to eat—grass cutting, dishwashing at a diner. It was a time of unemployment and cutbacks

134

everywhere, of inflation, and worst of all, moralizing by people whose morals he questioned.

Then Patrick stumbled onto The Book. The Book took bets on anything anyone wanted to bet on, from horse racing to football and baseball games, to what the last three numbers would be on the stock market totals, to whether Squeaky Fromme would be convicted for not shooting President Ford. Patrick got a job running errands for the mob that ran The Book. There weren't any risks involved. The Book had no trouble with the cops. The payoff was too good.

When he said that, Patrick gave Captain Roark a sly smile. "I learned long ago that the law protects the criminals if they're big enough," he said. "It's only creeps like me who can't spit on the sidewalk."

Errand running didn't make Patrick what he needed to support his appetite for women, booze, and an occasional joint. He started betting with The Book himself, at first just a two-buck bet on a horse. He won a little, lost a little. Most of all he listened. There is often a "sure thing" in betting situations, a fix, a sellout. He heard of one of these, begged, borrowed, and stole a couple of hundred bucks and came out with a cool thousand. This amused Ben Lackland, the head man of the mob who ran The Book. Patrick dribbled his winnings away pretty quickly. He heard of another "sure thing" and screwed up his courage to ask Ben Lackland if they'd trust him for a hundred bucks. They did, he lost.

He had a run of bad luck. Suddenly he owed The Book six hundred. Ben Lackland turned tough. He'd give Patrick a week to find the money, or else. Patrick put in a long-distance call to his father and was told to drop dead. He had no choice but to turn to Allegra. She was divorced now, working full time for Eliot Keyes, the man Patrick assumed was her lover. He was loaded. Patrick suggested to Allegra she could borrow it from her boy friend. Two days later she wired him the money.

"That would be chicken feed for a man like Keyes," Patrick said.

Quist knew it hadn't come from Keyes, but he couldn't say so because he couldn't say how he knew.

Ben Lackland, Patrick told them, was pleased. He liked Patrick and he was glad not to have to make an object lesson of him. Patrick began to have larger opportunities, opportunities to handle money, collect winning bets, deliver on losing ones. He was allowed to go in and out of the big walk-in safe in the offices of The Book. "Count off five hundred for Joe Busby," Lackland would say, "and deliver it to him."

Patrick began to see ways to skim a little gravy off the top. Everything was done in cash—no checks, no books, no records. He also discovered that the betting operations were a small part of the business done by The Book. They were loan sharks. They loaned money at exorbitant rates to people in trouble: businessmen, ranchers, city officials. And there was a strong-arm squad that enforced collections.

Patrick was looking for a big killing that would provide him with enough money to move on. One day he came across one of the "sure things," a heavyweight fight being held in Mexico City. Patrick lifted a package of bills, ten thousand dollars, from the walk-in safe at The Book. He didn't place his bet with The Book, because they'd guess where he'd found the cash. It was perfectly safe, he told himself. He'd spread his bets around and a day later he'd have collected his winnings and be able to replace the ten grand in the safe at The Book.

"Only the sure thing turned out not to be a sure thing," Patrick told them. "I was told that the favorite was going to take a dive. Maybe it was a manipulation by gamblers, maybe somebody forgot to pay the favorite off. Who knows? Mean-

136

while I was ten grand out of bounds and no way in the whole world to get off the hook. It took Ben Lackland about a week to catch up with the shortage."

There were no elaborate threats—just a simple one. Get it up in ten days or they'd use him for shark bait in the Gulf of Mexico.

"I put on the stupid-kid act for them," Patrick said. "What else could I do? I had no way to pay back the money. I'd work it out for them if it took the rest of my life. Lackland laughed at me. He said he'd run a check on me. He knew my old man had a solid job up here at the Sports Arena. That meant, Lackland said, that he had contacts with all kinds of rich and important people. It would be no problem for him to raise twenty grand.

" 'What do you mean twenty grand?' I said.

" 'I figure it may take a couple of weeks for you and your old man to work it out,' he said. 'The extra ten grand is the price of the loan.'

"I told him my father wouldn't pee on me if I was on fire. He just laughed and said he thought he would.

" 'We do favors for people up there, and people up there do favors for us,' Lackland said. 'One of them will visit your old man and explain we hold him responsible for your debt. If he doesn't pay we'll feed him to the New England sharks. You better help persuade him we don't fool around.'

"I told him I didn't have the bread to get up here. He said then I better walk. I had two weeks to get twenty thousand back into the safe." Patrick looked around. "Could I have a glass of water?" he asked.

Lydia went out into the kitchen and came back with a pitcher of ice water and a glass. The boy drank thirstily.

"I had enough bread for a bus ticket to somewhere in Ohio," he said. "And enough for a phone call to my father." He smiled, a crooked little smile. "Lackland's friends up here had already been to see him. I didn't need to explain it to him. I bet those phone lines are still hot. He told me to get here as fast as I could. I asked him could he do something about it? 'Not for you,' he told me, 'but I care about my own hide.'

"So I got here the morning after Allegra was murdered."

He just sat there after that, looking at Bonham and Quist.

"So you lied to me when you came to my office after your father was killed?" Bonham said. "You'd been here for three days?"

Patrick nodded. "It saved a lot of explaining at the time. Like I said, I got here the afternoon of the day Allegra was found. I—I didn't know she was dead till my father told me. I went to his office at the Arena. He told me. And then he beat up on me." Patrick glanced at Captain Roark. "He was over fifty years old, but if you think you're tough, copper, I'd like to have seen you tangle with him."

"So he beat up on you," Roark said, a muscle rippling along the line of his square jaw.

"And he seemed to enjoy it," Patrick said. "I mean, it wasn't like he was mad at me any more. It was like it was a sporting event. Artistic. He didn't cut me, but I felt like I'd been run over by a truck. And then he told me—he told me he'd found a way to make us all rich. A way to pay Lackland and leave 'something for everyone' is the way he put it."

"Did you ask him how?" Quist asked.

"I asked him but he wasn't telling. He just said, 'Meet me after Allegra's funeral on Thursday and I'll have the bread. You can fly back to Texas first class and pay the debt.' I was to come to his office again toward the end of Thursday afternoon. I went looking for him, but he never showed. Then he was dead."

"And you came to my office and pretended you'd just arrived," Bonham said.

"I had to find out if he had the money on him when you

found him," Patrick said. "Time is running out on me, Mr. Bonham. I won't get one day beyond the two weeks Lackland gave me. Now that he knows my father is dead he'll pay me off, just the way he promised. That's what I meant by a contract."

"Maybe he won't be interested in you," Roark said. "Maybe he already collected from your old man."

"And killed him?" Patrick asked, his eyes widening.

"Your father said he'd have 'something for everyone,' didn't he? Maybe The Book collected a hell of a lot more than their twenty grand," Roark said.

"And then risked going through Landis's office and his home looking for a photograph?" Quist asked. "It doesn't add up, Captain."

"How do you make it?" Roark asked.

"Landis took a picture of someone that was worth a lot more than twenty thousand dollars," Quist said. " 'Something for everyone.' He was going to collect it the morning of the funeral. Blackmail."

"No!" Red said softly.

"I think he went to meet his victim somewhere," Quist said. "Money for the prints and negatives. Only the victim killed him after he had what he thought he wanted. I think after Landis was dead the victim discovered that Landis had held out on him. There was another negative somewhere. That's what he's been looking for."

"And who is he?" Roark asked.

Quist turned away. "Someone I'm going to find and I hope crucify," he said.

"And what are you going to do about Patrick's problem?" Lydia asked.

Quist gave her an amused, one-sided smile. "The little mother of all the world!" he said.

CHAPTER TWO

Two A.M., the third day.

Neither Bonham nor Captain Roark seemed prepared to argue Quist's theory. But where to move for answers, for proof? Red Landis, in response to questions from Bonham, made it clear that since she had known Jim Landis, married him, he had rarely been out of the area, except for trips into the city to buy photographic supplies. A few times, on his day off—which was no specific day since the Arena operated seven days a week—they had gone into the city together to see a musical on Broadway. Pictures he had taken would seem to have been shot in Cranville, at the Arena, or in New York. The victim was almost certainly local. He had known where Landis's cottage was, where his office was.

"Red, think for a minute," Quist asked her. "Were there ever times when your husband seemed to be unexpectedly flush? Did he buy you presents for no particular reason? What I'm getting at is, were there times when he seemed to have a money windfall of some kind?"

Red shook her head, very positive. She had persistently rejected the blackmail notion. Not the man she loved. Not ever.

"It's just possible this was his first go at blackmail," Quist said. "His life had been threatened by the messenger from The Book. He had to raise a lot of money quickly, and that was the only way he saw to do it."

"He would have told me!" Red said. In addition to her physical beauty there was a dogged loyalty that must have drawn Jim Landis to her.

140

"He might not, Red," Quist said. "Telling you would have scared the hell out of you." He paused, frowning. "All the same that may be our man's next move. He hasn't found the missing negative. His next danger may be that Landis talked to his family about it. You, Red. Patrick. He may come back to ask you."

"If he does we'll be waiting for him," Roark said. "We'll have a man guarding your cottage, Mrs. Landis."

Red's dark glasses turned toward Patrick. "If you can stand being under the same roof with your father's whore, you're welcome to stay here," she said. "If they're protecting the cottage I think your father would want it."

Patrick looked sheepish. She had turned out to be something more than he'd expected. "I'm sorry I said that," he said. "You don't owe me anything."

"I know," Red said. "But I'm offering."

"It would help if we could protect you both in the same place," Roark said. "The best thing would be to put you both in protective custody."

"And our man would simply wait until they were finally let out of jail," Quist said. "He has to know by now that neither Red nor Patrick has talked to the cops. But that doesn't mean to him they don't know what it is he must hide. He can't be sure they won't try to use whatever it is against him, just as Landis did. If you don't leave your men outside the cottage with signs on them, Roark, our man may just walk into the trap."

"We're supposed to be the bait?" Patrick asked.

"You think of anything better?" Roark asked.

The daylight of that Saturday morning crept through the bedroom windows of Quist's duplex apartment on Beekman Place in the city. Quist lay on his back in the king-sized double bed, staring up at the ceiling. Lydia slept peacefully beside him, her dark hair spread out on the pillow. They had finally driven back to town and arrived at about three-thirty.

Quist turned his head to look at Lydia. He wondered how he had ever managed without her. He reached out and touched her, and she made a soft, loving sound in her sleep.

He threw back the cover, gently, and got out of bed. She moved restlessly and he thought she would wake. But she didn't. He went into the adjoining bathroom and stood under a steaming hot shower for a long time. Then he shaved, went into the dressing room and slid open the closet doors behind which were dozens of suits, jackets, slacks, shoes. Quist's wardrobe looked like the rack in a fashionable men's shop. Flamboyant dressing was part of Quist's personal image, but on this day he chose to be less attention-getting. A pair of plain gray slacks, a dark brown summer tweed jacket, cordovan loafers. From built-in drawers he selected a white shirt with a button-down collar and a brown silk-knit tie.

He dressed slowly, as though by not hurrying he would somehow recharge his batteries. He'd had only four hours' sleep each of the past two nights. He was just knotting his tie, thinking that fatigue made him look like a man with a hangover, when the aroma of fresh coffee drifted up from the floor below.

That Lydia!

She was in the kitchenette, wearing a pale yellow chiffon negligee. She had a bright red apron tied around her waist. She was broiling bacon in the oven. She looked back over her shoulder at Quist.

"Thought you could walk out on me, did you?" she said.

He took her in his arms and held her against him. She smelled, he thought, like fresh-mown clover.

"Two minutes," she said, when he finally released her.

"I'm going to check on Dan," he said.

Dr. Zukor was not at the hospital, but the private nurse Quist had hired for Garvey gave him a little better than a doing-as-well-as-can-be-expected report. Garvey's vital signs were stable. It was still too soon to know which way the tide was going to turn. The fact that the patient's condition hadn't worsened was a hopeful sign. Dr. Zukor had checked conditions about an hour ago and left a message for Quist. "Keep praying. Maybe it does work."

Lydia had brought his breakfast out onto the terrace that overlooked the East River: juice, bacon, eggs, gluten toast with sweet butter, coffee. She joined him, limiting herself to juice and coffee.

"Imagine your being able to cook, too," he said.

She watched him eat, pleased at his obvious enjoyment. Finally, when he leaned back in his chair and lit one of his long, thin cigars to go with his second cup of coffee, she spoke.

"You're not going to take me back with you today," she said. It wasn't a question.

"Exposing you once to our man is enough," Quist said.

"I want to be with you," she said.

"I know." He was frowning at the blue spiral of smoke that drifted up from his cigar. "It isn't as though we knew who he was, luv. If he thinks we're getting in his hair he may try to take us out, and we have no way of guessing where he may be coming from. The fewer targets he has, the better. I don't want you to be one of them."

"I could stay at the hospital with Dan. If he comes to—"

"Please, sweet. If I know you're here and safe I can concentrate on just one thing, finding the sonofabitch!"

"Do you have any ideas at all? Any really good guess?"

"None," he said. "I wish I knew who Allegra's lover was."

"You don't buy Jim Landis anymore?"

"The real Allegra Landis isn't the person Andrew described to us," Quist said. "We know now, from Patrick, that she had a lover before the marriage broke up. That's probably why Landis got the divorce. She let him have it on grounds of cruelty so that he wouldn't expose her man. That man is probably who she was with the night Andrew went there, listened, took off."

"Could Landis have taken pictures of them together at some time?" Lydia asked. "Is that what Landis had, evidence of a love affair?"

"Possible," Quist said. "If that was so we know two things about him. He's rich, able to pay a good deal more than twenty thousand dollars. 'Something for everyone.' He's strong—the way he beat Dan, the way he threw you down on the floor and taped you up."

"Eliot Keyes?" Lydia asked.

"He's probably rich enough. But he's sixty years old, a little overweight, man of distinction. You described the man in the ski mask as thin, wiry, strong. Not Keyes."

"So where do you begin, Julian?"

"Looking for a lost camera, looking for a missing negative —or, rather, the place where Landis may have hidden it."

"And you have less than two days if you're to help Andrew."

Quist's face hardened. "Helping Andrew is really secondary now. Getting even for Dan comes first."

"If that's the way it really is," Lydia said, "we'd better be ready to cut off the Crown campaign the first thing Monday morning. I could help Connie with that."

Quist stood up and moved around to her chair. He bent down and kissed her forehead. "God knows where I'll be, love. I'll try to keep in touch with Bonham's office in case you need to reach me."

For an instant her fingers gripped the sleeve of his jacket. "Take care, Julian," she said. "You're dealing with some kind of a psycho out there."

He patted her shoulder reassuringly. "Sometimes crazy people are easier to understand than the ones who claim to be sane. They don't take a phony moral stance."

*　　　*　　　*

In Cranville there was no news when Quist arrived there shortly before ten o'clock. He had a brief conversation with Dr. Zukor. Garvey was going to pull through, the doctor predicted, but whether his physical and mental equipment would be intact was a question. He was still comatose.

Bonham reported that Red and Patrick Landis were still at the dune cottage, under guard. No one had made any effort to get at them. Quiet was the name of the game since the man in the ski mask had ripped up the cottage twelve hours ago.

At the Arena the circus was preparing for its last two performances. Business as usual was the story there. Two brutal murders and a near third must not be allowed to interfere with the public's pleasure.

Quist drove slowly along the main street of the village of Cranville to the graceful old Colonial Rouse where Eliot Keyes had his office. The village, bathed in a warm summer sun, with the tang of salt in the air from the ocean, was a sleepy oasis, surely not the scene of bloody crimes. At the worst it had happened to "someone else," and was "no concern of ours." And yet, Quist thought, that was just an appearance. Behind those curtained windows there must be endless gossip. Some of it must point to what he was looking for, but how to get at it?

There was Mrs. Moffet, the gabby receptionist in Keyes's office. But she wanted him to talk. She was "in shock" over the Landis murders. "Poor Allegra" and "that husband of hers." Quist didn't satisfy her appetite for secrets.

Eliot Keyes saw his caller without delay.

"Is there any news of your friend, Mr. Quist?" he asked when Quist was ushered into his handsome office.

"You know about Garvey?" Quist asked.

"This morning's news on the radio," Keyes said.

"The doctor is hopeful," Quist said. "I need some help from you, Keyes."

"Of course. Anything."

"When I saw you before, I didn't ask you if Landis was at the funeral. I assumed he was. Now I think he wasn't."

"I certainly didn't see him there," Keyes said.

"But there were two girls from your office, friends of Allegra's, who were there."

"Yes."

"I'd like to talk to them. I'll put it on the line to you, Keyes. We believe Allegra had a lover. We believe he was with her the night she was murdered. It's vital that we identify him, get to talk to him." Quist looked for signs of shock, concern. If Keyes was the man, this should rock him. There was no sign of it.

"I find that hard to believe," he said.

"Patrick Landis knows she was having an affair before the marriage broke up. It was why he left town. But he doesn't know who the man was. He talked to Allegra about it. She admitted that there was someone, but she wouldn't name him."

"You believe the boy?"

"Yes. Now it's possible that women friends of Allegra's might know. There might have been private talk. After all, Landis did get the divorce. Close friends might have asked about that, might have gotten some sort of admission from Allegra."

Keyes pressed the intercom button on his desk. "Mrs. Moffet, please ask Julie and Marian to come in here." He leaned back in his desk chair. "It's hard for me to accept, Mr. Quist. I've known Allegra since her high school days. She was married the year she graduated. That marriage always seemed to be a great success. Landis settled down, seemed to become a solid citizen. The boys were born, grew up, loved and cared for by Allegra. I would believe that Landis might have played around on the side, but never Allegra. It just isn't in character."

"But we know that she was with a man the night she died," Quist said.

"My dear man, she was a free woman then, owed no loyalties to anyone. She was attractive. Prime of life, I'd say. No reason at all why she shouldn't have been having an affair. Nothing sinister about it."

"I'm not passing moral judgment on her, Keyes. I just want to know who it was, because he was there with her the night she was butchered by someone."

Mrs. Julie Anderson and Mrs. Marian Kraft came into the office and were introduced to Quist. Late thirties, early forties, Quist thought. Allegra's generation.

Keyes explained that Quist was part of the investigation of two murders and that the man who'd been beaten up at the Arena the night before was a business associate of Quist's.

"You were both at Allegra's funeral," Quist said, "so I assume you were more than casual office acquaintances."

Julie Anderson, a not entirely natural blonde, with a pert, upturned nose and bright blue eyes, conceded that she'd known Allegra most of her life. They'd played together as children, gone to school together, been friends after they were both married. "I was very close to Allegra."

Marian Kraft, dark, a person who prided herself on her neatness, Quist thought, had come to live in Cranville about a year after the Landises had married. She met Allegra here in the Keyes office during one of her part-time stints. She and her husband had done things with the Landises—movies, an occasional eating out together, parties at home.

"Allegra was really a nice person," Marian Kraft said. "Not gossipy, never mean about things. And Jim was fun. He used to say he was 'a reformed black sheep.' I thought they got on marvelously together, brought up their kids in a healthy way. I was stunned when they broke up."

Then Quist laid it on the line. Allegra had been having an

147

affair, which is why her son left home and probably why Landis had divorced her. She had obviously had a lover who was with her the night she was murdered. They had to identify him. Quist hoped there might have been some exchange of confidences that would help.

"Keeping her secret won't do her any good now," Quist said. "If you know something, it might help to get at her killer."

Marian Kraft was instantly all innocence. She'd never dreamed Allegra was unfaithful to Jim. She'd never heard a whisper of gossip about her. After her divorce Allegra had said she was suddenly the target for all the loose males in town, but that she wasn't having any part of it. Marian Kraft just didn't believe what Quist was suggesting.

"But, of course, Julie was closer to her than I was," she said.

Julie Anderson wasn't so quick or so glib. She looked bothered. "When we were kids Allegra and I had no secrets from each other," she said. "We told each other about all our crushes. In our senior year in high school she told me she was having an affair with Jim Landis. I was shocked." Julie laughed. "He was so old—twenty-nine! But there was something exciting about it. He had such a terrible reputation. But then they were married, and it seemed to work out so well for both of them." She hesitated. "I was married the next year and my husband, Dick, couldn't stand Jim Landis. Jim had boasted to Dick about all the women he'd had before Allegra. I think Dick thought I might have been one of them. He gave me a very hard time about it. I was not one of them, by the way. But I didn't see much of Allegra after that, except when she filled in here at the office. She never even hinted she might be having something on the side. But, when Jim divorced her, I asked her, point-blank. I mean, why would he get the divorce? She denied there was anyone, and that was that."

"And you believed her?" Quist asked.

"Why not? She'd never lied to me before. But after the divorce we began seeing more of each other. She was here on a permanent basis. We used to lunch together. My husband travels on his job and we spent some evenings together, mostly at my house because she hadn't settled anywhere at first. She told me what she told Marian—that suddenly men thought she was free and eager."

"Did she mention names?"

"A few. Charlie Spivak, who is known around here as the Cranville Stud. He's made passes at all of us in his time, I guess. Being married doesn't matter to Charlie. There was Ted Frost, who works at your Arena. There are some other names I won't mention because they're married men with families. She wasn't having any of them, she told me, and I believed her. She said she wasn't ready for a new adventure yet. She mentioned an older man who was very dear and sweet, who just wanted companionship."

Quist moistened his lips. "His name?" He guessed this was a reference to Andrew Crown.

"No name," Julie said. "When she got the Braden cottage through Mr. Keyes, I kidded her about it. I suggested that now she had a place where she could take on a lover in private. You understand, if I'd been in her shoes I'd have taken on a lover if I could find one. We were both getting to the age when it would be now or never. She laughed and said there were dozens of people living on the estate within shouting distance of her cottage. She said there was less privacy there than anyplace you could imagine."

"And she didn't hint to you that there was someone?" Quist asked.

"Quite the contrary. She made it clear there was no one," Julie said.

"And yet there was," Quist said. "She'd stopped telling you the truth."

"Or simply not telling me what was none of my business," Julie said. "One thing I can tell you about Allegra, Mr. Quist, she wasn't hopping into the hay with anyone who turned up. If she had a lover, she'd have been completely loyal to him. She would lie to me about his existence, protect him from any kind of hurtful talk. She was a one-man woman."

"Until toward the end of her marriage when her son discovered there was more than one," Quist said.

"Let's say she was a one-man-at-a-time woman," Julie said.

"But you have no idea who that one man could have been?"

"I'm sorry, Mr. Quist."

Quist begged the use of a phone and called Bonham's office. The detective wasn't there but a secretary told Quist that a Mrs. Andrew Crown had been calling him all morning. It was urgent.

Quist called the Crowns' number and got Andrew.

"It seems Marjorie has been calling me," Quist said.

"Both of us, you might say," Andrew said, his voice lifeless. "I've decided to withdraw from the election race, Julian. If you can possibly take the time, there are important details to discuss before—before I go to the police."

"Police! What the hell are you talking about?"

"If you could come over here, Julian—"

"I'm on my way," Quist said. "And don't go impulsive on me till I get there."

"This time I'll tell you the whole truth, Julian," Andrew said.

That was something of a stunner. In all of this tangled mess Quist had felt the one thing he could be certain of was Andrew Crown's complete honesty. "The whole truth—" What had Andrew left out of his story?

It took about ten minutes to drive from Keyes's office to

150

the Crown house overlooking the Cove. Andrew was waiting for him at the front door.

"Beautiful day," he said, as though he meant it.

Quist thought he was looking at a man relieved of tensions. That in itself was unexpected.

In the entrance hall Andrew asked for news of Garvey. Quist gave it to him. Hopeful but still some doubt about total recovery.

"I feel guilty," Andrew said. "I dragged you into this. I feel responsible for what happened to Dan and Lydia."

"Don't be a dummy," Quist said. "Now what's all this about going to the police?"

Andrew led the way to the room Quist had thought of as Marjorie's sitting room. She was there, sitting in her surrounded wheelchair, looking very handsome, very bright, very proud.

"Good morning, Julian," she said. "You lied to me, you know." She didn't sound angry.

"Lied to you about what?"

"You said there was no other woman."

He gave her a faint little smile. "I said there was no woman —on earth. A literal truth, Marjorie. It wasn't my secret to divulge. But I gather Andrew has told you."

Andrew had moved to the wheelchair and his hand rested on her shoulder. "The truth is a miraculous thing," he said. "I decided—well, that there was no way to go on without it. Thanks to you, Marjorie seemed ready to start living again. I couldn't build a new beginning on secrets from Marjorie. I had to risk bringing it all out into the open."

Marjorie reached up and touched her husband's hand. "I drove him to whatever he did, whatever he felt, by being such a self-pitying bitch," she said.

Quist had seen this sort of thing before. People who make up a quarrel, or who come together after a long separation, can't keep their hands off each other.

"So I'm delighted—happy for you both," Quist said. "But what does that have to do with your campaign and with going to the police?"

"I can't let you go on risking your neck for me," Andrew said.

"We have a day and a half left before the campaign is supposed to open," Quist said. "And if I am risking my neck it's not for you. I want the guy who clobbered Dan, and I want him racked up permanently. Will revealing to the police that you are the man Nancy Braden saw at the cottage that night do anything to catch the killer? I say it won't. As a matter of fact it will divert them. They'll waste time horsing around with you."

"The problem is, Julian," Marjorie said, "Andrew didn't tell you all that happened that night."

Quist's pale eyes turned as cold as two newly minted dimes. "Well, perhaps it's time," he said.

"Please, Julian, it's not that I lied to you," Andrew said. "It—it's just that I didn't tell you all of it. Everything I did tell you was gospel truth. But—but there was more."

Quist stood perfectly still, not speaking. Marjorie gave her husband's hand an encouraging squeeze.

"It happened exactly as I told you—all the way," Andrew said. "I heard what I told you I heard when I arrived at the cottage that night. I—I ran out of there, just as I told you, and encountered Mrs. Braden. I took off. It was almost dark, which explains why her description of me was so vague. And I did drive around, just as I told you—but not for as long as I let you think."

"You went back there?" Quist asked, his voice hard.

Andrew told it haltingly, his tensions returning. He had driven away from the cottage after his brief encounter with Nancy Braden. He was in an emotional turmoil—hurt, angry. He felt cuckolded. He had let Allegra make a fool of him. He felt shame and guilt for what he had let himself do to Marjorie. He felt like an old fool. He drove round and round as he had told Quist, but not for so long a time. After an hour or so he decided to go back to the cottage and have it out with Allegra.

"But I didn't want to run into anyone this time," Andrew said. He was holding Marjorie's hand tightly now. "I drew my car off the main highway, and decided to go to the cottage through the woods at the back of it. If—if the man who had been with Allegra was still there, I wasn't going to make a big scene with him. But if he was gone, I intended to have it out with her.

"The Bradens keep those woods very nicely cared for. I mean, they don't allow the brush to grow up. It was easy to get to the cottage because there was a light burning in that kitchen room, just as it had been the first time. The upstairs was dark. I told myself the man must still be there. But I felt I had to have it out with her. I went around to the front of the cottage and knocked on the door. No one answered so —so I let myself in. The door wasn't locked.

"I must have been out of my mind, Julian. I listened and there wasn't a sound from upstairs. I—I slammed the door. I thought if they were up there I'd hear someone move. They'd be startled by the slamming door. There was nothing, no sound. Then I called out to her. 'It's Andrew!' I said. 'If you can't see me, just call out to me and say so!' No response. I went to the foot of the stairs and turned the light switch that lit the upstairs. That would stir them up, I thought. Nothing happened. And so—and so I went upstairs. I suppose there was some kind of morbid fascination involved. I guess I was pretty sick just then. I would see the place where she'd betrayed me, the bed where she'd been making love to someone else. Well, there was no one upstairs. The bed—the bed had been stripped."

"Stripped?" Quist interrupted. He had expected something else.

Andrew nodded slowly. "Knowing what we know now, you thought I was going to tell you of some evidence of a bloody violence. There was nothing like that, Julian. The room was neat as a pin. The only odd thing about it was that there were no sheets, no summer blanket, no bedspread on the bed. There were two pillows, but no pillowcases. It didn't make any sense to me then and it doesn't make any sense to me now—unless—"

"Someone took away bloodstained evidence of a killing," Quist said in a flat voice.

"It must have been that," Andrew said. "The police haven't told you that's how they found the room?"

Quist frowned. "I don't think anyone mentioned the condition of the room," he said. "I don't think I was bright enough to ask. They said they'd gone over the cottage for fingerprints and found nothing. But not anything about the bed being stripped."

"Someone did a meticulous job of cleaning up the place," Andrew said.

"Is that all you didn't tell me?" Quist asked.

Andrew let out his breath in a long sigh. "No," he said.

"Well, let's have it, Andrew."

"I didn't have any reason to think of any kind of violence," Andrew said. "I just assumed Allegra had gone off somewhere with the man she'd been with—probably to have a drink somewhere, or a late supper. So I decided to leave. I wasn't going to wait for her to come back. I guess—I guess I'd run out of steam. I wanted to get out of there. I suddenly knew I didn't want to see her then or any other time. It was over. It had really been over days ago. I began to be reasonable about it, I think. She'd turned me down and she had a right to do anything she chose to do. She didn't owe me any sort of loyalty. I'd been a silly damn fool to get so worked up about it."

"I'd left him with no life," Marjorie said softly, reaching

154

up to touch her husband's face.

"Well, I started away from the cottage the way I'd come, through the woods," Andrew said. "I'd only gone a few yards when I heard someone—a heavy footstep, misstep by someone, and a muttered swearing. Then silence."

"You didn't see who it was?" Quist asked.

"No. And I didn't want him to see who I was. I didn't want to answer questions. After I'd waited a few moments I took a few steps forward. Instantly I heard him move—away from me." Andrew's voice was unsteady. "It was a crazy kind of hide-and-seek, except that we were both trying to hide from each other. When I realized he wasn't trying to find me, I just bolted for my car and drove away."

"And you never saw him?"

"No."

"Do you think he got a good look at you?"

"It was dark, very dark. I don't think he was ever close enough to identify me."

"He could have found your car before he came into the woods," Quist said. "He could have gotten the license number."

"I suppose so. But if he did, why has he kept still about it?"

"You haven't received any threats? It would be a perfect setup for blackmail, particularly when the news broke the next day."

"There's been nothing," Andrew said.

Quist moved impatiently across the room and back. "You didn't look for Allegra in the pond?" he asked.

"Good God, Julian, why should I? I didn't dream anything had happened to her."

"Why didn't you tell me this in the beginning?" Quist said. He was angry.

"I don't know, Julian. I think I was ashamed of having gone back there. It didn't add anything of importance."

"The hell it didn't! Don't you realize there may be two people now who can place you on the scene that night?"

"The next day, when the news broke, I thought that man wouldn't want to be placed there any more than I did. I just wasn't making sense, and I'm sorry, Julian. But Marjorie and I have talked it out and decided I should go to the police with the whole story."

"I don't think I agree," Quist said.

The Crowns waited for him to explain why. He sensed they wanted him to be right.

"For selfish reasons," Quist went on. "Bonham and Captain Roark will focus on you for—for how long? A day, two days? All that time Dan Garvey's attacker will be burying himself out of sight. You'd be a red herring I don't want you to be distracting Bonham and Roark. My conscience is clear about it because I know you haven't killed anyone, Andrew."

"But if people find out later I withheld information—?"

"What information have you withheld, chum?" Quist asked. "You can't identify the man in the woods. The police don't have to be told there was someone around. They know that. The police know Allegra was involved with a man that night. They're trying to find out who he was. But you can't help them. You don't know. So telling them you were there —twice—will only muddy the water and get them investigating you, which will waste time."

"And the campaign?" Marjorie asked.

"If we haven't broken the case by Monday morning, I think you'll have to call it off, Andrew, or delay announcing that you're running."

"Delay for what reason?"

Quist glanced at Marjorie. "Your wife's health," he said. "She's taken a turn for the worse."

Marjorie smiled at him. "Just when I've gotten well?"

"I can't use Marjorie," Andrew said.

"You will," Marjorie said. "If Julian thinks delaying the

announcement is the right course, I'm going to be suddenly very ill on Sunday night."

"I can't let you—" Andrew began.

"Be still, Andrew," she said, reaching out to him. "I love you. I'm looking forward to living with you in Washington."

CHAPTER THREE

On the way back to Cranville from the Cove, Quist found himself about to pass St. Peter's Cemetery. There were two big stone pillars with iron gates thrown open, the entrance for funeral hearses and cars. Quist slowed down and turned in.

The cemetery occupied a sloping hillside. Some of the first gravestones he saw were obviously very old, some dating back to Revolutionary War days. Over the years the people of Cranville had been buried on higher and higher ground. The whole place was immaculately cared for grass mowed and trimmed, some tombstones with little flower plantings around them.

Fifty yards inside the gates Quist stopped the Mercedes. He could hear the sounds of a power mower somewhere off to the right. He walked toward the sound. The caretaker was an elderly man, gray-haired, who walked with a limp behind his mower. His face was tanned a leathery brown. He stopped the mower and turned off its motor as he saw Quist approaching. He seemed to be glad of an excuse to stop working. He mopped at his face with a red bandanna handkerchief.

"Help you?"

Quist introduced himself and explained who he was.

"That's a hell of a thing about Landis," the old man said. "I'm Joe Mullins. Been pushing this mower and ones before it that weren't so good for damn near thirty years."

"You knew Landis?" Quist asked.

"Sure I knew him," Mullins said. "He grew up here in town. Wild kid, but he seemed to have settled down."

"The cops talked to you at all about Landis?" Quist asked.

"Oh, sure," Mullins said. He leaned on the handle of his mower. "But I wasn't on duty the night Landis was found, lyin' on his wife's grave. Jake Porzelt was on that night."

"Isn't it unusual in a small town like Cranville to have a night watchman at the cemetery?"

"I suppose you'd say so. But we've had a rash of like vandalism here at night; gravestones turned over, marked up. A lot of towns along the coast have had it. Kids, we think. No sense to it, but sort of disgusting molesting the dead, I say."

"I understand Porzelt didn't hear any shots that night. Did he see anything unusual?"

"No, but you can't be everywhere at once."

"The police have a theory that someone killed Landis— somewhere else—hid the body all day, and then brought it to the cemetery at night in a car," Quist said.

"Maybe. But he didn't drive a car into the cemetery."

"You sound positive about that. He could have driven in without lights. It was a clear night, wasn't it?"

"He couldn't have come past the gates in a car," Mullins said. "They're closed after dark, locked on the inside."

"But there's no trouble getting over the stone fence on either side of the gate. Someone could have carried the body in."

Mullins shrugged. "Possible but not probable. Landis was a big man. Hoisting him over the fence and carrying him up the hill would be quite a chore. Mrs. Landis's grave is near the top. With Porzelt looking for trouble, it doesn't seem like it could be got away with."

Quist changed his tack. "You were on the job here the day of Mrs. Landis's funeral?"

"Sure. I have to oversee the grave digging," Mullins said.

"Were you actually at the funeral?"

"Standing by."

"Did you see Landis here?"

"No. The cops asked me that."

"But he could have been here, couldn't he, somewhere up the hill watching?" Quist knew Andrew had been there, somewhere, watching.

"Possible," Mullins said. "But if he was, I didn't see him."

Quist paused to light one of his long, thin cigars. Landis had almost certainly planned to meet his blackmail victim that morning. He'd have wanted to hold that meeting on some kind of neutral ground. The cemetery would have been ideal. He'd have a reason for being there if he was seen and later asked about it. His ex-wife's funeral, representing his sons; that would be a solid explanation if anyone had a reason for asking.

"An idea has been growing on me," Quist said to Mullins. "Suppose Landis was here, was killed here that morning. The Medical Examiner says he was killed right around the time of the funeral—just before, during, or just after. The killer hides the body here in the cemetery, comes back after dark, puts the body on the grave. He might not have to carry it very far."

"No chance," Mullins said positively.

"Why?"

"Look around you, Mr. Quist. The cemetery is wide open. No shrubbery, no place to hide a body. I make three or four rounds of this place every day. Made at least two after the funeral. You couldn't hide an apple in here I wouldn't notice. It's my job to notice anything unusual."

"Absolutely no place to hide a body?"

"Absolutely no place."

Quist looked slowly around, the cool breeze off the ocean ruffling his blond hair. "What about that?" he asked, pointing to a mausoleum, built to look like a small gray stone house.

"No way," Mullins insisted. "Cranville is a small town, and people don't bury their dead in a showy way these days. That mausoleum belongs to the Tichenor family, and if you look at the date on it you'll see some Tichenor was buried there back around the Civil War. There are three other what you could call walk-in tombs here and that's it."

"But they'd make ideal places to hide a body, wouldn't they? You don't look inside them every time you make a round, do you?"

"I haven't ever looked inside any of them," Mullins said. "They're locked. Families, if they're still around, have keys, I suppose, and Ed Peabody, who's head of the Cemetery Association. I can tell you this. None of the doors to those four mausoleums has been forced or damaged. First thing we thought of when the vandals showed up here. They'd be ideal, we thought, for kids who wanted to have sex, or smoke pot, or whatever they do. They were never touched."

"I wish I could get a look inside them," Quist said.

"You'd have to go to Peabody for that. He's a real estate agent in town."

"Well, thanks anyway," Quist said.

"No sweat," Mullins said. He shook his head. "Funerals aren't what they used to be, you know. Mrs. Landis was well known, well liked from all I hear. But hardly anyone came to see her off. Only when you got an organization behind you does anyone come—a church, the Rotary, the Legion. There'll be a big crowd to see me go because I got this knee in World War Two. The Legion will see to that. But Mrs. Landis gets zilch, because there's no organization behind her."

"I guess it didn't matter to her," Quist said. "She wasn't able to count the house."

"Yeah, I guess," Mullins said.

The crowd for the last circus matinee was gathering at the Arena when Quist arrived there. Ted Frost wasn't in his office but his secretary made a telephone available to Quist. He called the hospital. There was nothing new on Garvey. Perhaps it could be called a slight improvement. Every hour you didn't go backwards was a plus.

Lydia was alive and well and living on Beekman Place—and worried about him. The office was having its problems fending off questions about Andrew Crown's campaign from backers, the press, a speaker's bureau, the Monday Today Show.

"Stall where you can," Quist said, "but if the heat gets too hot you can let it slip that Mrs. Crown's health may delay the announcement."

"Oh, I'm sorry," Lydia said.

"Don't be," Quist said. " 'The truth will set you free.' Andrew spilled the entire beans to Marjorie and you might say they're second honeymooning. Marjorie is prepared to be very ill tomorrow night if we haven't nailed our man and still need to hold off."

"Julian, something tells me I wish you weren't out there," Lydia said.

"Something?"

"Intuition, if you like. I've had some kind of an ice cube in my stomach all day. Your man strikes so quickly, so savagely when he has to. Can't you leave it to Bonham and Roark, come back here and worry about the campaign?"

"Dan wouldn't sit on his hands if I were in his place," Quist said. "I feel—like someone playing blindman's buff. If I could just reach out in the right direction, I'd put my hand on him. He's that close! And he's here, not in New York, love."

"I know when it's useless to argue with you, but take care, my darling."

Quist's next call was to Bonham. This time he found the detective in. He had to ask his question carefully. Had there been nothing at all in Allegra's cottage, in her bedroom in particular, that gave them any lead at all to the killer?

"It keeps haunting me that he must have left some kind of clue. There must have been a considerable mess there. Allegra was stabbed—how many times? There must have been bloodstained sheets, bloodstains all over the place, bloody fingerprints perhaps."

Bonham sounded surprised. "Didn't I tell you? The bed had been stripped clean; no sheets, pillowcases, blanket, or bedspread. We thought it was odd. The whole room looked as if it had just been manicured by a spring cleaner. We looked for sheets and pillowcases in the washing machine in the kitchen. Nothing there. Plenty of clean stuff in the linen closet."

"He had all night to clean up the room I suppose," Quist said. "He could have washed the sheets, ironed them, put them in the closet."

"Pretty bizarre idea that he'd hang around like that. Probably took them away with him," Bonham said.

"What about Allegra? She was nude when you found her?"

"Yes."

"No nightdress, negligee anywhere?"

"Clean things in her closet. Nothing we could say she wore at any time that night. Between the house and the pool we found a few bloodstains. The pool was red with her blood. But the cottage itself was so clean you wouldn't believe it. Somebody really went over it."

Quist changed the subject. He outlined the theory that

he'd put to Joe Mullins at the cemetery—that Landis had been killed there, the body hidden in one of the four mausoleums, and then dragged out after dark and placed on Allegra's grave.

Bonham whistled. It was an idea that hadn't occurred to him. "I'll get Ed Peabody to open them up for me. You could be right. We might find something helpful."

"I'll be in touch," Quist said.

At that point Ted Frost came into the office. He had his first box office reports from the matinee audience.

"I heard from a lady that you were one of Allegra's suitors," Quist said.

Young Mr. Frost looked embarrassed. " 'Suitor' isn't exactly the word," he said. "I told her I was just the right prescription for a lonely chick. She laughed and said if she ever felt sick she'd let me know. There was nothing heavy about it. It was a no, and I didn't want it enough to fight a war to get it."

"When was this?"

"Oh, months ago. I was talking to Landis one day and said I had a need for a little white meat. He said his ex-wife was playing the field and might be just what I was looking for. He gave her high marks for her bed techniques. So I tried. No dice."

"He seems to have been something of a sonofabitch," Quist said.

"Oh, it was all very light. Sort of joking." Frost frowned. "It seems she said yes to the wrong guy."

Quist moved away again. "Red Landis told me her husband was working on some kind of security system for the Arena. What was it?"

"There was something," Frost said, "but I don't know exactly what. Steve Bateman, our security chief, could tell you."

"Where will I find him?"

"He's always in the main arena when there is any kind of show. We have the usual run of creeps: pickpockets, drunks, goons starting fights, lost kids. Any usher can point him out to you."

The circus was in full swing. The audience, seventy percent kids, was charged with delighted anxiety over a trapeze act. Quist asked an usher and Bateman was pointed out to him, a square man with a brown crew cut, wearing a gray tropical worsted suit that Quist's practiced eye told him was cut to hide a shoulder holster. He walked over to Bateman and introduced himself. Bateman's cold gray eyes lighted a little.

"You're Dan Garvey's partner, aren't you? How is he doing?"

"We're hopeful," Quist said.

"Dan got me my job here, you know," Bateman said. "I'd like to get my hands on the bastard that got him!"

Quist remembered that in the first day of the Arena, Garvey had asked Lieutenant Kreevich to recommend some cop who would like to take on the Arena security.

"Mark Kreevich recommended you," Quist said.

"You know him? Great guy. Best detective I ever saw on the force. Too bad we haven't got him out here about now."

"Dan was trying to get some information about Jim Landis when he was slugged," Quist said. "I'm following up for him."

"Landis was a good man at his job," Bateman said. A girl in flesh-colored tights somersaulted through the air, high above the Arena floor, to be caught by a partner, hanging head down from a swinging trapeze. The children groaned and screamed. "Ties knots in my guts to watch that," Bateman said. "You have to be crazy to make a profession of it. I said Landis was good at his job, but I had the feeling he was always on the make."

"Women?"

"No, no, not that. Something bigger than his job—fast money, big money. I said someday he'd make it and leave us flat. Instead he got a hole in his head."

"Was there something about a security system of some sort?"

The kids were all standing, applauding and screeching. The trapeze act was over, and in the center ring three trick riders appeared with two big gray horses that began to canter around the ring at a rhythmic pace.

"Landis was clever," Bateman said. "I didn't mean that big money would come from something off-color. He invented things. He was a camera buff, you know. I figured he might come up with something in that field he could patent and make a fortune out of. He had something cooking and he showed it to me."

"Oh?"

"There's something—I think it's called the Owl Eye System—that some banks and corporations with big security problems use. It's like a camera that can take pictures in the dark without any flash. Infrared something or other. You walk into a bank vault at night, or some restricted area in a plant, say, and the Owl Eye will take a picture of you without you ever knowing it. I saw one once when I was covering a bank job in the city. It's fairly bulky. It's got a tube about two feet long. Lens on one end, screen on the other. Well, Landis had a refinement on that. It was a little job, like a hand camera. A watchman could carry it, hear something, take a picture of it without exposing himself to people with guns or maybe bombs."

"Are you telling me that Landis had a small camera that could take pictures in the dark without a flash?"

"Sure. Damn good pictures. He showed me some. He took them of some of the offices here in the Arena when they were dark. Every detail clear as a bell."

Quist felt his pulse beat a little faster. Pictures in the dark!

165

Pictures of a murder? Pictures of someone dragging a naked woman, running blood, and throwing her into a lily pond? Pictures of a killer?

"He built the camera himself?" Quist heard himself ask.

"He had a little workshop on the second basement level here," Bateman said. "But that was ripped apart just like his office by someone."

The killer seemed to have covered all the bases and, presumably, come up empty. Quist decided to let Bateman in on it. He outlined the theory that Landis had been blackmailing someone, that the blackmail victim had killed him thinking he had all the prints and negatives he needed to be safe. Afterwards he must have discovered there was a negative missing.

"I assume it's a negative," Quist said. "He must have had a print without a negative to match it, else why the frantic search here and at the Landis cottage?"

"Sure," Bateman said. "He had to have a print without a negative or he wouldn't have known he didn't have it all."

"Now you tell me about this camera that can take pictures in the dark without a flash," Quist said. "You see what it suggests? Landis could have been somewhere around his wife's cottage the night she was killed, gotten a picture of the murderer and the murder, the disposal of the body, the works. For that you'd kill a man because he could put you in jail for the rest of your life. Landis held out one just to be sure he was safe."

"And the killer didn't find out until he'd committed his second murder," Bateman said. "It adds up, Mr. Quist."

"If we could find that negative we'd have our man. Case closed." A muscle rippled along the line of Quist's jaw. "But where in God's name did he hide it? Not in his office here or his workshop. Not in his cottage. There must be a thousand places in the Arena where he could have hidden it."

"Ten thousand places, a hundred thousand places," Bateman said. "A little piece of film? It could be stuck under a seat, and there are fifty-five thousand of them right where we're standing. There are three basements below this, the club and the offices above it, the lofts, the broadcasting studio. What would it be, two inches square, no thicker than that?" Bateman held his thumb and forefinger almost together. "Jesus, Mr. Quist, if I had an army to look for it we might hunt for months, forever, and not find it."

"And we have no reason to be sure it is here," Quist said.

Bateman was watching a pretty girl doing a handstand on the rump of a galloping gray horse. "A blackmailer usually has a way to protect himself," he said after a moment. "He usually makes it clear to his victim at the payoff. He's passed on a copy of the evidence, or a piece of the evidence itself like this negative, to his lawyer, a friend, a member of his family. If anything happens to him that lawyer, or friend, or member of the family will go to the cops with it."

"But no one has," Quist said.

"Let's say I have that negative, that Landis gave it to me," Bateman said. "I'm supposed to go to the cops with what he's given me, something in an envelope, say. He might not have told me what it was. So he gets murdered. I decide to look at what I've got before I take it to Bonham. It's a negative, a picture of someone hacking away at Allegra Landis with a butcher knife. If I give it to Bonham, the killer has had it. But if I decide to use it for myself, bleed the killer of all he's got? Why not? I'd be getting even for my friend Landis and feathering my own nest at the same time."

Quist's smile was bitter. "He didn't give it to you, did he, Bateman?"

Bateman laughed. "Maybe I wish he had."

Quist found himself buying Bateman's theory. Landis had turned over the incriminating negative to someone who was supposed to go to the police if anything happened to him.

Now that someone had the murderer by the short hairs. Quist felt so damned close! A lawyer, a friend, a member of the family, Bateman had suggested. Landis's victim was supposed to pay off the twenty thousand dollars Patrick needed to settle with The Book, and there would still be "something for everyone." Now that lawyer, friend, or relative could keep going to the well until it was dry, unless he, like Landis, underestimated the savagery of the killer.

There was only one source of information about lawyers and friends and family, and Quist headed the Mercedes toward the dune cottage where Red and Patrick were still being guarded by the troopers. One of the men on duty was one of the troopers who had picked up Patrick in the grounds the night before. It seemed he'd just checked in after having been relieved to get some sleep. Quist glanced at his watch and saw that it was close to three o'clock.

Red Landis, looking almost cheerful, opened the front door to his knock. She was wearing a mini-skirted cotton print dress that revealed her extraordinarily good legs. Behind her in the living room, which had been pretty well put together again, Quist saw Patrick sitting at a card table. The two of them had been playing backgammon. So much for earlier hostility. Red saw his surprise.

"You have to pass the time someway," she said. "Wow, am I glad to see you, Julian! There's been nothing on the radio or the TV, and those jerk troopers won't give us the time of day. What's happening? How is your friend Garvey? Where is Lydia? Can I get you a cup of coffee?" The words tumbled out of her, nonstop.

Quist accepted the offer of coffee, reported on Garvey and Lydia. He had a feeling that Patrick was not nearly as relaxed as Red, who came back from the kitchen, still prattling about the lack of news. She looked completely refreshed. Quist doubted that Patrick had had much sleep. His red-rimmed eyes seemed sunk in their sockets.

"Patrick owes me four million, three hundred and thirty thousand dollars," Red said, laughing. "He's a lousy backgammon player. We play for very high stakes since we're only kidding."

"I need help from you two," Quist said. He outlined the path he was traveling. Landis had taken a picture of the murder with his no-flash camera, had tried to blackmail the killer, made a deal and been killed after he turned over prints and negatives. But he had held out one incriminating negative.

"That's what your ski-mask friend was looking for last night," Quist said. "What he was looking for at the Arena when he slugged Dan. Now we think Jim may have turned that negative over to someone to hold for him, to turn over to the cops if anything happened to him. Tell me, Red, did Jim have a lawyer?"

"What did he need a lawyer for?" Red asked, obviously confused by Quist's outline. "I mean, he didn't have a business where he needed a lawyer."

"Who got his divorce for him?"

"Oh, that was Bob Lewis. He's local. A nice guy."

"Would he know who it was Allegra was having an affair with while she was still married to Jim?"

"Gee, I don't think so, Julian. Jim never told me even. The grounds were mental cruelty. Allegra didn't fight it. They got it out of state because I guess New York doesn't go for mental cruelty."

"Were Jim and this Bob Lewis close enough for Jim to trust him with confidential matters?"

"I think they hardly knew each other," Red said. "I think Jim just picked him out of the phone book when he wanted a lawyer for the divorce. Oh, maybe he knew him from around town."

"What about close friends?"

Her face clouded a little. "Not anyone really close since

I've known him," Red said. Her lips trembled. "I mean, I guess I was his number-one friend."

"And he never gave you anything to hold for him?"

"No! Wouldn't I have turned it over to the police if he had?"

It all had the ring of truth. Quist turned to Patrick. The boy was sitting quite rigidly at the card table, his hands gripping the arms of his chair.

"How about you, Patrick?" Quist asked. "Did your father turn over anything to you?"

"No! I came here looking for money last night, as I told you. He said he was going to collect the day of the funeral and I thought he might have. I've had it now, don't you see? The Book isn't going to let me up."

"You got here from Texas a couple of days before your mother was killed. Right?"

"Right."

"You went to your father and found he'd already been threatened by The Book. Right?"

"Right."

"Did he tell you how he thought he might raise the money?"

Patrick tugged at his short brown beard. "He said he had no way to raise it. He was mad—and scared. He said he didn't know anything but to go to Allegra. She worked for Eliot Keyes, a rich man. Through the office she was in touch with a lot of rich people. She'd raised some bread for me before."

"Six hundred dollars, hardly the kind of cash you needed now."

"My father said he didn't know any other way. I was to lie low for a few days and then check back with him. Then —then I heard on the radio somewhere that Allegra had been murdered. Do you know, I thought maybe he'd done

170

it? If she'd turned him down, he just might have done it, I thought. But then, when I went to see him he was all smiles. He certainly didn't look like a killer. He said he'd have what I needed and something left over for everyone the day of the funeral."

"And he gave you something to hold for him?" Quist asked in a conversational tone.

"He gave me—what the hell are you talking about?"

"With instructions to turn it over to the police if anything happened to him?"

"No! He gave me a few bucks to eat on until the payoff."

They stared at each other for a moment and then the boy looked away. His hands were unsteady as he lit a cigarette.

"I can't make you tell me the truth, Patrick," Quist said. "I know you're in a bind. If you don't come up with twenty thousand dollars The Book will exercise its contract on you. If you go to the police with that negative you use your last chance of raising the money yourself. But I warn you, if you try to blackmail this killer he won't hesitate to pour it on you. He's gone too far to stop at another killing."

"Patrick!" Red said, wide-eyed. "You don't have any negative, do you?"

"No! No! *No!*" Patrick was up out of his chair, storming across the room.

"You're the logical person for your father to have left it with," Quist said. "He could trust you because you needed his help."

"*No!*"

"Are we just playing with words, Patrick? Did he tell you where he had hidden it? Is that why you came here? Have you found it and are you just waiting for the cops to get off your back?"

"For God sake, will you let me alone!" Patrick shouted.

CHAPTER FOUR

"It fits together like a Chinese puzzle," Bonham said. "The only trouble is we're missing the piece with the face on it."

Quist had driven directly to Bonham's office from the dune cottage and laid his whole theory on the table. Bonham was right. They had everything but a face and a name. Somewhere there was a negative, taken by Landis with his no-flash camera, that had that face on it. Quist was willing to bet that Patrick had it or knew where it was.

"We could go over there and sweat it out of him," Bonham said.

"I don't think so," Quist said. "The boy is almost hysterical with fear. His life is on the line. The only thing in the world he's sure of is that The Book will carry out their threat. He thinks he has a way to get up the money, and dangerous as it may be, illegal as it may be, he isn't going to throw away his chances just to be a good guy or a good citizen. He has no one to turn to. His mother's gone. His father's gone. His brother would have no way to help. No, I don't think he'll talk, no matter what kind of pressure you put on him."

Bonham stared glumly at his steepled fingers. " 'The music goes round and round and it comes out—' where?" he said. "We have it all but the only thing that matters—the name of the man who was Allegra's lover that night she died, who may have been her lover since before she was divorced. Who may have been the grounds for that divorce. Let's put it down in order." He began to check off on his fingers. "Patrick comes to town for help. His money or his life is the name

172

of the game. He goes to his father, not because his father would willingly do anything for him but because his father has been threatened by The Book. Landis says he doesn't know where to get help unless it's Allegra. She has a rich boss, and rich contacts. And so Landis slips away from his job. No one saw him go so everyone assumes he was somewhere at the Arena. He always carries a camera, and this time, since he was going somewhere at night, he carries the one that takes pictures in the dark. He arrives at the cottage to ask for help and is in time to see someone lugging Allegra's dead body out to the lily pond. She was dead when she was thrown into the pond, you know. No water in her lungs. He takes pictures, and the killer has no idea of it. Landis sticks around and takes pictures of the cleanup, perhaps the guy carrying away the bloody sheets and pillowcases, the bedding. I think it's fair to say that he knew who the man was. He goes home eventually and develops his film. He has himself a gold mine. He knows who the man is and he knows he's got more than enough money to handle the problem—a hell of a lot more than enough. 'Something for everyone.' "

"He was full of cheer and happiness when he told Patrick he had it made," Quist said.

Bonham went on. "So now he sends some copies of the prints to the killer, announcing that he'll call him on the phone. When the killer sees what Landis has on him he has to decide what he's going to do. Landis calls him on the phone, sets a price on the merchandise. A meeting is arranged. The killer's house, some lonely stretch of road, the cemetery, as you have suggested. They meet. The killer shows his money. Landis shows more prints and the negatives. Time for the exchange. But the killer guesses that he'll never be off the hook. There'll be other prints hidden somewhere. Out comes his trusty forty-five and he shoots Landis between the eyes. He hides the body somewhere—in his house, in the trunk of his car, in a mausoleum at the cemetery. At night he drapes the corpse on Allegra's grave. Perhaps while he's waiting for nightfall—because this all happened in the middle of the day—he goes over what Landis brought him. There may be more prints, he knows, but now he sees that there is one negative missing. There is a damaging picture, but no negative to match it. He has to find it. He has to find extra prints if there are any. He probably thought of Bateman's lawyer, friend, or member of the family. But nothing happens. He goes to the Arena. Now here we come to a sticky part, Quist."

"He couldn't run around the Arena during a matinee of the circus wearing a ski mask."

"Right," Bonham said. "He must have known the routines. That everyone would be at the main Arena level during a show. I have to think he knew he might be recognized but no one would question his being there. But he ran into bad luck—Garvey. He knocks Garvey out and he knows he then has time to make a thorough search. But it produces nothing.

"The dune cottage is something else again. He can't be seen going there, couldn't explain it. Which, I suggest, means a lot of people in Cranville would know him by sight. He has to wait till after dark. Then he puts on his ski mask, gets in, trusses up the girls, and again takes his time searching. No luck." Bonham sighed. "So that's the scenario, as they say in Washington. What does he do next? What would I do if I were in his shoes? Just wait to be blackmailed by someone else, and kill again?"

The phone on Bonham's desk rang and he answered. Then: "Oh, hello, Ed. Thanks for calling. Yeah—yes, that's good. *Who?*" A long silence while Bonham listened. Then: "Yes, I guess we could get a court order. Well, thanks very much, Ed."

Bonham put down the phone and stared at Quist, his eyes cold and opaque behind his glasses. "That was Ed Peabody, the Cemetery Association. He got permission from three of the families who own those mausoleums to open them. The fourth family refused. Don't want the peaceful dead disturbed. It's an outrageous request." A nerve twitched at the corner of Bonham's mouth. "Care to guess who that family is?"

"No way I could guess," Quist said, and suddenly had an idea as he said it.

"The Caldwell family," Bonham said. "Incidentally the Caldwell mausoleum is quite close by Allegra Landis's grave. It was built for old man Caldwell, and his daughter now speaks for the family."

"Nancy Braden!"

"The one and only," Bonham said.

Slim, wiry, strong, Lydia had said about the man in the ski mask. That would fit Rooster Braden perfectly. Rooster Braden, known by everyone in town.

"Can you get a court order to open the Caldwell mausoleum?" Quist asked.

"Yes, when I can find the right judge—who's probably out on a golf course somewhere on a Saturday afternoon," Bonham said.

"Peabody's warned the Bradens, if we're right about the mausoleum," Quist said. "You find the judge. I'll go out to the Braden place and try to keep them occupied for a while."

Both men were suddenly standing.

"Watch your step," Bonham said. "Braden must be pretty desperate if he thinks we're on his trail."

The late afternoon sunshine bathed the countryside in a relaxing warmth, but Quist, driving the Mercedes up the winding, wooded road that led from the highway to the Braden estate, felt as if his bone marrow was chilled. They had, he was certain, found the piece of the puzzle with a face on it. John Braden—Rooster Braden. And yet there was something about it that surprised him. He had written down

175

Braden as a tough, cool customer, who would have his own way, no matter what. No messing around, no avoiding the issue. The one savage blow to the back of Dan Garvey's head, in character. A kind of cold, efficient violence. But the seven or eight stab wounds inflicted on Allegra suggested an inefficient hysteria that didn't seem to fit Rooster Braden. It was, for Quist, a troublesome inconsistency. Braden out of control, Quist thought, was more frightening than the efficient Braden.

The Mercedes emerged from the woods—woods in which Andrew Crown had played hide-and-seek in the dark with someone who was probably Jim Landis, taking his pictures —to the lovely vista of fields and paddocks, grazing horses, and the gray stone stable complex in the distance. The tranquillity of it all seemed somehow sinister to Quist, knowing what he now knew. Or did he know anything? Were he and Bonham just guessing?

In the work ring near the stable someone was schooling a big, black gelding. From a distance Quist thought it was Braden. But as he came closer, he saw that it was Nancy Braden, dark hair blowing loose around her shoulders. He remembered thinking that Rooster Braden, riding Golden Belle, had looked like a centaur, man and horse all of a piece. Nancy Braden was almost as good, Quist thought as he watched her. She was riding the black horse at a steady canter, making a figure eight that forced the horse to change leads. It was a simple maneuver but handled with grace and excellence. He had thought of her as a petulant, angry woman in their one meeting, but on a horse she was poetry in motion. That must have attracted Braden to her—in addition to the Caldwell money.

Quist pulled the Mercedes up alongside the training ring, and Nancy Braden recognized him and walked the magnificent black horse over toward him. She sat her saddle, erect yet relaxed, patting the horse's neck.

"Well, Mr. Quist," she said. There was a mocking note in her voice. "Here to talk about another nonexistent international jumping contest?"

"It couldn't exist, Mrs. Braden, until we had some ammunition. Your husband is, we hope, the kind of ammunition that might sell the idea."

"I think you're playing detective," Nancy said, "and I've had a stomachful of detectives."

"A friend of mine is fighting for his life in the Cranville hospital," Quist said quietly. "Yes, I'm trying to find out who attacked him, if you call that playing detective."

"Well, you certainly won't find his attacker here," Nancy said.

"That isn't why I came," Quist said.

"Oh?"

"I know you've been asked by the Cemetery Association for permission to open the Caldwell Mausoleum at St. Peter's, and that you've refused."

"And will continue to refuse, Mr. Quist. The police have messed up my life for the last few days. I will not have them disturbing my dead father. The mausoleum hasn't been broken into, so how can they hope to find anything there?"

"In this day and age the best locks can be picked," Quist said. "We think Landis's body was hidden somewhere close to his wife's grave. There is no place to hide it out in the open. The Caldwell mausoleum is the most logical place. If it wasn't used, then nothing will be disturbed. If it was, you would want to know, wouldn't you?"

She still sat erect on the horse, stroking the shiny black neck. Her forehead was creased with a deep frown. She was, Quist thought, wrestling with alternatives.

"The County Attorney can get a court order, you know, Mrs. Braden," Quist said.

"I didn't want it opened," she said sharply. "I still don't want it opened. But if Johnny thinks I should—"

"Can I talk to him?" Quist asked.

Her tongue moved along her lower lip. "He's working with Golden Belle down in one of the lower fields," she said. "Brush jumps."

"If you'll point out the way," Quist said.

"You can't get there in your car," she said. "If you want to walk down, just follow that fence line. You'll come to another pasture which you can't see from here, and below that is where Johnny is working Golden Belle."

"Thanks," Quist said. "I'm sorry to have bothered you, but it's really quite important."

"Whatever Johnny says, I'll go along with it," Nancy said.

Quist got out of his car, climbed a fence, and began walking briskly in the direction she'd indicated. The first field was about two hundred yards long. He climbed the fence again and went down a steep embankment to the second field. Looking back he saw that he was out of sight of the barn as she had said he would be. He began walking down the sloping meadow to where Braden should be schooling Golden Belle. Then he heard the thunder of hoofs on turf behind him. He turned and saw Nancy coming toward him on the big black horse at a full gallop. She had evidently decided to be in on the conference with her husband.

It wasn't until she was almost on top of him that he realized she meant to run him down!

He made a quick turn to his right, felt a searing pain in his ankle and went down on his hands and knees. Instinctively the black horse leaped over him and he heard the woman screaming curses. The horse, jerked back on his haunches, was turned and headed toward Quist again, full gallop.

He tried to run and realized his ankle was too badly sprained to give him any mobility at all. It was like some kind of bizarre movie close-up, the woman's white teeth bared as she slashed at her mount with her crop.

Quist stood up and made an unsteady lunge for the bridle. The horse reared, pulling his head free. Quist fell and, looking up, saw the great iron-shod hoofs coming down on him. He rolled away, but not quite quickly enough. One hoof grazed his shoulder, and he felt as if he'd been hit with a sledgehammer.

The horse sprang forward again, the woman yanking at his mouth to turn him. Quist, almost helpless, staggered up, standing almost literally on one leg, clutching at his shoulder. Cold sweat was streaming down his face and inside his shirt.

She came at him, lashing at the horse. The animal was not a killer, his instinct told him to avoid the man, but he was being whipped into a lathered frenzy. Quist hopped to one side, but was not agile enough to avoid that slashing crop that cut across his face. He went down on his hands and knees, tasting his own blood. She had gone past him by nearly fifty yards before she could turn the horse for another assault.

He knelt where he was, not able to move. There was no way to resist, no way to escape. This time she would have him and that would be that.

Then he heard someone shout.

"Nancy! *Nancy!*"

He lifted his head, and through eyes that were fogged with sweat saw another horseman bearing down on him. It was Rooster Braden on his Golden Belle. Together they would crush him into hamburger. He found he couldn't take his eyes off the two racing animals that were converging on him. The last thing he would ever see were those flaring nostrils, those flying hoofs, and the woman leaning forward over her horse's neck, teeth bared, murder in her eyes, crop flailing.

And then, five yards away from him, the two horses collided. The black horse staggered, knocked off stride, and went down, the woman screaming hurtling through space.

Golden Belle neatly jumped over Quist and galloped on.

Quist shook his head like a punched-out prizefighter. Nancy lay in the clover-scented grass a few yards away from him. Rooster Braden had dismounted and the two horses galloped away in the direction of the barns.

Braden walked over and knelt beside his wife. He examined her with hands that seemed expert. Falls from a horse were nothing new to him. Then he did an extraordinary thing. He sat down beside Nancy in the grass, took a cigarette out of his pocket and lit it. The bright dark eyes turned to Quist.

"Broken neck," he said in a matter-of-fact tone. "Maybe it's better that way."

Through a kind of dazed fog Quist realized that the collision of the two horses had not been an accident. Rooster Braden had deliberately ridden his wife off the kill.

After that there were more voices shouting, and looking up the rise of the ground Quist saw Bonham and Captain Roark running toward them, followed by a couple of stable hands. Rooster Braden saw them, too, and like a very tired man, lay back on the grass and stared up at the fleecy clouds, tinged with sunset colors. Quist wondered if the man's life was on parade up there in the sky.

Roark reached them first, and seeing that Quist was at least alive knelt beside Nancy Braden. Then he stood up. "She's dead," he said.

"She was thrown from her horse," Quist said.

Braden turned his head, his lips twisted in a wry smile.

Bonham reached Quist, whose clothes were disheveled and dirt-smeared, whose face had the bloody mark of Nancy's crop across the left cheek.

"What the hell happened to you?" Bonham asked.

"The lady tried to ride me down," Quist said. "I think Braden saved my life. You must have found something or you wouldn't be here."

Bonham nodded. "A few pieces of a smashed camera in the Caldwell tomb," he said. "The print of a photograph, kicked away out of sight. They must have missed it when they tried to clean away signs. The picture shows Mrs. Braden dragging Allegra's body through the woods."

Braden turned his head again. "Nancy killed them both," he said. "I—I tried to cover up for her." He took a deep drag on his cigarette and tossed it away into the grass. "Isn't there a better place than this to talk?"

It was hours later. Quist was stretched out in a deck chair on the terrace of his Beekman Place apartment in New York. Lydia sat on a cushioned stool beside him, holding onto his hand as though she thought he might evaporate if she didn't make sure.

He had limped into the apartment, his clothes a mess, his face scarred. He was numb with fatigue.

"It's all over," he told a startled Lydia.

Before he could tell her, he had to get out of his clothes, stand under a steaming hot shower, dress in slacks and a beach jacket. He had come back downstairs barefoot because it hurt him to wear a shoe on his injured foot and ankle. He had made himself a double Jack Daniel's on the rocks and they had gone out on the terrace where he sat looking at the twinkling lights of the city, sipping his drink. Each swallow seemed to bring him a little nearer back to life. Finally he looked at Lydia and smiled.

"Ready?" he asked.

"I'm half dead of being ready!" she said.

"It's easier and more logical to begin with something to which I don't have all the answers," he said. "It's the story of a quarrel and a love affair. I don't have all the answers because Allegra and Jim Landis are dead and can't tell us."

It began with the day Allegra met Rooster Braden about

a year and a half ago. It was at the Arena. She had evidently gone there to see her husband, and in the parking lot, on her way out, she couldn't get her car started. Braden was there, riding in a horse show. He tried to help her get the car started without any luck. He offered to drive her somewhere and she said she'd be grateful if he'd drive her home to the dune cottage.

"Braden says she was in some kind of emotional state," Quist told Lydia. "She couldn't hold it in. Her husband was a bastard, she told him. They had had the quarrel to end all quarrels. She didn't care if she never saw him again. Parenthetically, I can only guess it was some quarrel over the boys. Braden, when he got her to the cottage, made a pass at her. He says now it was completely unlike her, but she was in such a rage at Landis, that she said yes, just to get even. And so they made love—and they were both lost. Braden says it was not like anything he had ever imagined. Didn't Allegra use the word chemistry to Andrew? Well, this was a chemistry for them both that swept them off their feet.

"Allegra fought it when he came back the next day It shouldn't have happened; she had only given in because she was so angry at Landis. But she owed him fidelity. There had never been anyone else. But when Braden touched her there was no resisting. This is what we used to call a 'grand passion.'

"Braden couldn't get free—or wouldn't get free—to marry her. His whole way of life was built around Nancy's money. So Allegra undertook a clandestine, fiery affair with him, totally against her own principles, her own code of ethics. He would come to the cottage when Landis was at work. One day Patrick found them out, without knowing who the man was. Allegra admitted to an affair, but she couldn't give it up. Then Landis found out about it and demanded a divorce. Nothing mattered to Allegra but to keep hold of Braden.

182

Eventually, maneuvering through Eliot Keyes, she was allowed to rent the cottage on the Braden estate. She was available whenever Braden wanted her. And yet—all the time—something in her wanted out. It wasn't her style. But she was like an alcoholic. One touch of his hand and she was gone.

"At some point Andrew came into her life. I think she may have thought the way out might be another man—good, kind Andrew. She tried to make it work, but in the end she knew, if she gave herself to Andrew, Braden would only have to whistle and she'd rush back to him. And so she sent Andrew away.

"That night when Andrew came back to plead once more and heard the sounds of lovemaking, he rushed out of the house and came face to face with Nancy Braden. It was too dark, you remember, for Nancy to identify him. I don't think any of us ever asked what Nancy was doing wandering around in the dark. Of course the fact is she had stumbled on the truth. She waited for Braden to leave his love, and then went into the cottage and butchered her!"

"Dear God," Lydia whispered.

"The wild stabbings were the frenzy of a jealous woman," Quist said. "But a very cool customer. It must have taken her a couple of hours to drag the body to the pool, go back to the cottage, clean it from top to bottom, wash the bloody bedclothing right there in the cottage washing machine, and then go back to her own house and tell her husband what she'd done to his mistress. She knew her man. He'd never turn her in. He needed her for all the things that made his life worth living. As we know now, Landis had gone to the cottage to get help from Allegra for Patrick, and for him, too, because he was threatened by The Book. He took pictures, God knows how many, of the whole horror."

"And almost got caught at it by Andrew," Lydia said.

"Landis developed his pictures, which would hang Nancy Braden to the highest tree. He sends prints to them and demanded—would you believe a quarter of a million bucks? 'Something for everyone.' The Bradens couldn't say no. They had to deal. The cemetery was ideal. Both parties had business there—an ex-husband, and the current landlords. Landis was to meet them at the Caldwell mausoleum with the prints and negatives, they'd have the money.

"To cover themselves Rooster Braden was to appear openly at the funeral while Nancy was to pay off Landis in the mausoleum. I think Braden thought that was all that would happen, a payoff, the incriminating prints and negatives in their hands. He hadn't properly assessed Nancy's psychotic state. He faces Landis in the tomb, looks at the prints and negatives, and then, before he can warn her that he had held out a negative for insurance purposes, she shoots him dead. The momentum of killing was on her.

"Braden had to help her cover. They went back to the cemetery in the evening, waited for dark, and then draped Landis's body over Allegra's grave, trying to make it look like suicide. Then, with time, they go over what they'd taken from Landis and find a damaging print without a matching negative. Braden had to try to find it. He knew the set-up at the Arena. He'd been there as a performer. He knew the dune cottage. He'd conducted a love affair there for months."

"But he didn't find it?"

"At the Arena he had just gone into Landis's office when he heard a key in the door lock. He just had time to switch off the lights and hide behind a filing cabinet. Dan came in, turned on the lights, sat down at Landis's desk to see what he could find, and Braden bushwhacked him with his gun butt. He was cool enough to stay and carry out a thorough search. We know what happened at the cottage later."

"And he came up empty again," Lydia said.

Quist nodded.

"Where is the negative, then?"

"Oh, Bonham has it," Quist said. "That's the District Attorney's case."

"Where was it?"

"In the cottage." Quist grinned at her. "Patrick came there to look for money, just as he said. But when he heard all the talk about negatives, he had an idea. That's why he was willing to stay there with Red, whom he despised. In one of the bathrooms there was a loose tile. When he'd lived there with Allegra and Landis he discovered it and used it as a hiding place for pot he was smoking. Landis discovered it, beat up on Patrick. But Patrick knew he'd remember it when he had something small to hide. Patrick found the negative there when we'd all left, but he had to stay put. The troopers were guarding the cottage, keeping him safe. He saw the possibility of saving himself from The Book by trying a little blackmail of his own. With Nancy Braden dead and Braden under arrest, he turned it over to Bonham. It was no use to him any longer."

"What will happen to him?" Lydia asked.

"I think the F.B.I. may be willing, even eager, to help him out with The Book."

"Why do you suppose Braden tried to save you, Julian? Thank God he did, but why?"

"I think he saw there was no end to Nancy's psychotic drive. It would be me, and then someone else, and then someone else. Of course he didn't mean to kill her. That was a sheer accident; the horse's misstep and fall, the way Nancy landed when she was thrown."

Lydia was silent for a moment. "What's next for us?" she asked.

"On Monday morning we launch Andrew Crown's cam-

185

paign for the United States Senate," Quist said. He smiled at her. "Meanwhile there is tonight and tomorrow in which to indulge in a grand passion of our own."

She touched his cheek with cool fingers. "What are we waiting for?" she asked.